They had an
for each othe

"I though you said you were hungry," Catherine murmured, snuggling up to Sam's sheet-clad length.

"I am," he said, his hand moving to cup her breast. Gently he tugged at the nipple, sending heated messages through her body.

Catherine's breath caught in a gasp. "Then, er, how about letting me up, so I can fix breakfast." His touch was doing crazy things to her senses, turning her insides to jelly.

"No," he answered in a lazy drawl.

"No?"

"No." With a rakish grin he pulled her beneath him. "I haven't had my fill of this banquet yet...."

THE AUTHOR

A Woman's Choice marks the second
book in a trilogy that began with
The Will and the Way. Author Rita Clay
Estrada has taken Sam Lewis from the first
novel and paired him with Catherine Sinclair,
a controversial character from an earlier
romance. Rita is now working on the
third book of the series—Leo's and
Brenda's story.

This talented author lives in Texas with her
husband, James, and their four children.
She also writes as Rita Clay and Tira Lacy.

Books by Rita Clay Estrada

HARLEQUIN TEMPTATION
48—THE WILL AND THE WAY
72—A WOMAN'S CHOICE

These books may be available at your local bookseller.

Don't miss any of our special offers. Write to us at the
following address for information on our newest releases.

Harlequin Reader Service
P.O. Box 52040, Phoenix, AZ 85072-2040
Canadian address: P.O. Box 2800, Postal Station A,
5170 Yonge St., Willowdale, Ont. M2N 6J3

A Woman's Choice

RITA CLAY ESTRADA

Harlequin Books

TORONTO • NEW YORK • LONDON
AMSTERDAM • PARIS • SYDNEY • HAMBURG
STOCKHOLM • ATHENS • TOKYO • MILAN

Published August 1985

ISBN 0-373-25172-6

huskily. She dabbed at the liquid gems that fell to her cheek only to glisten with brilliance before being absorbed into the tissue. She gave a dainty sniff and Sam's stomach lurched again. His radar was telling him to stay away from her, but the rest of him was out of control, grumbling with beginning hunger . . . for her.

It shocked him.

He leaned back once more, making a pyramid of his fingers and staring at a point on the far wall just above her head. He hoped he looked cool and controlled. He hoped he looked bored. He hoped he didn't look like a damned idiot drooling all over her!

Glancing at his watch, he cleared his throat. He was due in a meeting with his partner, April Flynn-Sullivan, in just a few minutes. That meeting couldn't come soon enough for him, he thought wryly.

Catherine Sinclair was probably the most beautiful woman he'd ever had sit in his office. She was also one of the hottest stars in Country and Western music. And she was lethal when it came to men, if her reputation was anything to go by. So, who could blame him if he was hot under the collar and a little in awe of her?

"I'm sorry, Mr. Lewis. I don't usually act this way," she said softly, forcing him to look at her once more. The moment he did, he was caught in her sapphire-blue gaze. Her silk blouse was the same unusual hue, catching the highlights and making her eyes seem brighter, deeper, more sorrowful. The pristine white of her suit and wide-brimmed hat accented the intensity of that blue.

He gulped. "It's quite all right. Now, can you tell me anything more about the diamond necklace? Where did

1

"I COULD HAVE BEEN KILLED, and the police didn't even care!" the tearful voice said dramatically.

Sam Lewis leaned back in his leather desk chair and scrutinized the beautiful blonde sitting across from him. She was crying her heart out, and all without a blotch or blemish, a runny nose or ugly expression. In fact, the tears made her gorgeous blue eyes appear to sparkle like just-polished jewels. What was he supposed to do? Take her in his arms and comfort her? Admonish her for being too attached to a necklace of perfectly matched diamonds? Tell her he was sorry, but this problem was out of his jurisdiction and she would have to find another attorney? He did none of these things. Instead, he frowned, feeling a faint queasiness in the pit of his stomach. The woman was beautiful, famous and making him extremely nervous—and he wasn't sure why. Only the sound of her sniffles and the leisurely whirling of the brass-and-wicker ceiling fan could be heard. Sam unconsciously let out his breath, unaware until that moment he'd been holding it.

Opening a drawer in his desk, he took out several tissues. "Here, Miss Sinclair," he said, with a roughness he didn't mean, as he pushed the small white pile across the desk toward her. "When you calm down, we'll talk."

"Thank you for being so patient," she answered

you keep it? In a safe or chest? Where was its location before you noticed it missing?"

"It was on the dresser, where I had dropped it when I returned from the party. I'm staying in a rented house my agent found. I was told that no one had the key, yet when I came out of my bath, the necklace was missing. Someone must have come in while I was there and stolen it!" She shuddered at the thought of another person being in the house when she was all alone. So did Sam. "Anyway I called my attorney in Dallas, and he recommended that I see you."

"What makes you think someone has a key? Are you positive you locked the doors behind you when you came in?"

"Yes. Well..." She sighed. "I'm not sure. I was so exhausted at the time."

"When did you call the police?"

"Immediately." Her eyes hardened into blue diamond chips. "They arrived over twenty minutes later!"

"What did the police say?"

"They thought that I might have given my key out to someone at the party that night! Can you imagine?"

Sam could imagine very well. Catherine Sinclair had a reputation for having affairs with wealthy men. She had once been a Texas millionaire's mistress for three years. What was his name? Oh, yes...Noah Weston. Funny, but she didn't look like what he would expect a mistress to look like. She was all soft and sweet and almost cuddly. There were light-purple smudges under her eyes, as if she needed a good night's sleep or perhaps a vacation. But Sam felt that she might well possess a will of iron underneath that facade, and that was what scared him. Was this on the level or was she trying to get away with stealing her own necklace for the insurance money? Was Catherine Sinclair in some type of money trouble? Or could this be a publicity stunt? Regardless, it wasn't really his problem and he needed to get that point across as quickly as possible so she could find some other attorney to handle this.

He cleared his throat for the third time since she had walked in. "I'm afraid that this is out of my realm, Miss Sinclair, but I can recommend someone who could look after this without any trouble. I'm in the corporate end of the law, and my partner is in family; so as much as we'd like to help you out, this is not our area of expertise. What you really want is someone who can mediate with the insurance company so they have the complete story." Had that sounded blunt enough? Too blunt? None of the above? He didn't know.

Her eyes welled with tears again. "You're sending me to someone else, and I'll have to go all through this again." She looked straight at him, her eyes telling him that she was mentally exhausted and not ready to face another ordeal. But he had no choice.

"I'm afraid so," he muttered, cursing himself for his reluctance to cut their meeting short. Reaching for a pad on the side of his desk, he said, "But I'm sure you'll find Leo Coulter very helpful. He's an excellent attorney." He scribbled the name and number of his good friend on the pad, tore off the paper and slid it across the desk.

She didn't move to pick it up. "And what happens if that person, whoever he is, returns to rob me again?"

"I doubt that he will. He probably didn't expect anyone to be there. He found a door open, saw your necklace and ran."

Catherine stood, displaying her perfect, full-blossomed

figure for his perusal. "I hope you're right, Mr. Lewis. My life could be riding on it."

A twinge of apprehension flew through him, leaving a dampness under his arms and across his forehead. Was he right or was he sending her out there to get robbed, raped or worse? No, he was panicking because she had a pretty face and perfect body. It didn't figure that a burglar would be stupid twice.

"Do you have a gun?"

"Yes."

"Is it registered with the police here?"

"Yes."

"Then keep it handy if it will make you feel better."

"I will."

"Good." He stood and cleared his throat once more. What on earth was the matter with him that he was acting so awkwardly? He walked around the desk and toward the door, escorting her out with what he hoped was gentlemanly, but professional, reserve. She stepped past him and began to walk across his reception area, and his eyes riveted on her delightfully feminine swaying hips.

She stopped as she reached the outer door, glancing over her shoulder to catch the expression on his face, which he was sure looked like slobbering hunger. A deep slow flush began at his neck and reached up to tint his cheeks and forehead. He was blushing like an adolescent schoolboy caught sneaking a peak at the pretty teacher's cleavage.

Her smile was slow in coming, her blue eyes crinkling in the corners as she intimately surveyed him in turn.

"Thank you anyway, Mr. Lewis." Her look might have been sensuous, but her voice sounded so sad and lonely that he wanted to say to hell with his warning radar and tell her to come back.

But he didn't, and she left, quietly closing the door behind her. He stood, his mind in a turmoil over his unaccustomed reactions to her.

"She wouldn't have to sing a note and the audience would still be captivated by her." His secretary's voice cut through his musings.

He shook his head ruefully. "Including this member of the audience," he said.

Brenda grinned, her freckled face lighting up with laughter. She had been with Sam a year, but he felt as if he had worked with her forever. She was around his age, divorced, and wanting to stay that way. Under those conditions it was easy to allow a good friendship to blossom. It was a perfect arrangement. "What did she do to you in there? Pull out a flute and hum a few bars of the cobra waltz? You look like you're under a spell."

"I need to get out and meet more people. I'm leading too sheltered a life. Compared to her, I'm so naive that she almost had me convinced I was in love," he joked, only he wasn't laughing. That was really funny, for he didn't believe in love at first anything, let alone with a woman of her experience and background. Her kind of woman was poison.

"A sheltered life? Meet more people? What is this, 'The Fairy-Tale Hour'?" Brenda's brows rose disbelievingly, and Sam grinned. He was on the town more often than anyone else she knew. Sam was constantly busy, doing something or being with someone, owning more cards that gained entrance to charity groups and clubs than she could keep up with.

"Maybe I'll change my habits, and then I'll come after you, Brenda. You'd better watch out."

"If that's a leer on your face, you'd better practice more. It looks a lot like agony," she said, still chuckling as she rolled a sheet of paper into her typewriter. "By the way, April was looking for you. I told her you were in a meeting."

"Damn!" he muttered under his breath. He turned back to Brenda. "Tell her I'll see her after I make a phone call. Then get hold of this attorney in Dallas for me." He held out a slip of paper. "His name should be in my index file. Let me know when you have him on the line."

After Sam closed his office door, he walked across the Persian-carpeted floor to the window, hands in his pockets, to stare out at the boulevard below. His back was to the room he had worked so hard for: the one that had the small gold plaque on the door that read Sam Lewis, Attorney-at-Law.

A late bloomer, it had taken him six long years to achieve that title, four of which were earned in this office as a paralegal for his partner while he worked toward his degree. And here he was, at thirty-seven, in the spot he had always imagined himself. He was supposed to be on top of the world. Vietnam was behind him, college was finished, his earning capacity had quadrupled, life was as he had always dreamed. He didn't need a blond monkey wrench in his life, screwing up the works now. Still, the lady definitely needed help. . . .

The phone buzzed and he reached over, flipping the On button. "Mr. Hannover? This is Sam Lewis in Los Angeles. I'm calling regarding a client of yours, Catherine Sinclair."

"Oh?" The gruff voice chuckled. "You calling to thank me for your new client or to put a hex on my next case, in retaliation?"

He laughed at the man's words. "I'll withhold judgment until I'm sure just how lethal she is. Can you fill me in?"

"Oh, geeze, what a loaded question." Mr. Hannover's voice held a sigh. "I'm not sure I can help you much. I don't agree with most people as to what makes Catherine Sinclair tick."

"Give me something. All I know is that she's dynamite, was another man's mistress and is out here to do a movie. Is she having financial problems? Last night her diamond necklace was stolen, and she believes that the insurance company is trying to prove that she did it to herself. Is there any chance she could have stolen her own necklace?"

Hannover seemed to hesitate a minute before answering. "Anything's possible, but I doubt it. The necklace has a matching bracelet worth just a little less. If she wanted to lose something, I'd bet it would be the lesser of the two, except that she loves both those pieces. It could be a publicity stunt of some kind, but I can't see her doing that, not after her last brush with the law, in which she was a witness for the state in a drug case involving a senator. Besides, for all her showmanship, she's a very private person who would rather not call attention to herself. It wasn't always that way, but, well. . ." His voice trailed off. "I'm also well aware of her financial situation and she certainly doesn't need the money. She's loaded. So, if you're looking for a snap judgment, I'd say she's telling the truth."

"Why?"

"Because for the six years that I've known her, I've only seen her lie outright once, and I really believe it was in desperation. A last-ditch effort to keep her millionaire boyfriend."

A flash of jealousy zipped through Sam and caught his breath in his throat. What was the matter with him that he should be jealous of another man he had never met? "Your good opinion of her doesn't seem to be universal. Her reputation is, uh, shady to say the least."

"I know, but only some of it is deserved. Look, if a man had done some of the things she has to get ahead in the music world, he would have been labeled assertive. But she's a woman, so she made enemies of other women and quite a few men along the way, including the press. The only piece of advice I can give you is not to judge her by what you've read or heard. I have a feeling that there's more to Catherine Sinclair than any of us know. You're going to have to wing this one."

"You sound a little enamored yourself."

"Not me!" he said with a chuckle. "I just don't happen to be as prejudiced as some others. I'm also lucky enough to have old age on my side, and at my age, my wife's about all I can handle." There was a note of pride in his voice when he said that. "I just see Catherine a little differently than most, because I worked with her on some tough legal problems. She's had to struggle twice as hard as anyone else to get where she is today. I admire the woman as long as she doesn't cross me. I also feel just a little sorry for her."

"Why?"

"No way." Hannover chuckled again, a rasping sound that almost grated the wires. "No more clues. You make up your own mind. I don't want to prejudice

you one way or the other. So you'll have to take her as
you see her. Besides, you don't have to handle her. You
could always send her to someone else. I figured that if
you didn't want to work with her you'd know somebody who would. I didn't mean to throw you a curve."
The older man's voice was noncommittal, telling Sam
that he knew more than he was saying.

"The information you just gave me could have probably come off a press packet." Sam's voice was dry.

"That's more than I had when I met her."

"Thanks a lot."

Sam hung up the phone and stared at it for a minute.
He had been right to get the case out of his office. Catherine Sinclair was not a woman he would be able to work
easily with, no matter how much money he would make.

He flicked the intercom to Brenda. "Remind me to call
Leo this afternoon and fill him in on Catherine Sinclair."
At least he could do that much for her.

"Yes, sir!" Brenda rejoined, barely keeping the chuckle
from her voice. Leo was Sam's friend and fellow attorney
whom Brenda had yet to meet, but his voice and manners
on the phone told her he probably led the same, woman-
filled life that Sam did. Birds of a feather . . .

"And let April know I'll be right in." His voice was
harsh, irritated with the women in his life reading him
so well. Dammit! Were all women the same?

CATHERINE SINCLAIR SLUMPED into a booth at the Polo
Lounge. Her hands were still shaking, and her short,
shallow breathing was making her dizzy. She had to get
over this fear of returning to the house. It was just a
house, just a necklace, just a freak set of circumstances,
she kept telling herself.

The waitress came up and she quietly ordered Perrier water with a twist of lime, then leaned back and held her breath to will away the dizziness. She had to get a hold on herself!

Two men sitting on stools at the bar turned to smile at her. She ignored them. The last thing she needed in her life was another man, especially after the fiasco with Noah Weston. The very last thing. She'd learned her lesson well enough the first time.

When the waitress brought her drink, she asked for a phone. It was brought to her table immediately, and she dialed a number from her small black address book.

"Tommy? Catherine." Her voice sounded strained even to her own ears. "I went to the attorney's office, and he said he couldn't help me. I have to see another attorney."

"Catherine, baby, don't worry," her agent breezed over the line. "Chances are it was a fluke that the burglar entered while you were there. No thief wants to be caught in the act. He won't return, I promise you," he said, his voice booming so loud she had to hold the receiver away from her ear. "Listen, baby, I talked to the studio. You'll have the script in your hands by the first of the month. The walk-throughs will begin two weeks after that. So, that gives you six weeks before you have to show up at the studio. You'll have time to rest up. You looked exhausted this morning. Make those circles disappear, Kitty, or we won't have a snowball's chance in hell of convincing them you're gonna make a *great* movie star. And, call me if you need anything." Without a goodbye or so long, he hung up the phone.

Catherine cradled the receiver and stared into her drink. She refused to allow the tears that stung her eyes to fall. Her hands still shook, her body was cold. What was the matter with her? Was she so exhausted that she saw old ghosts where there were none, imagined hurts and feelings where none existed? Was she insane or was she so mixed up that she should be stretched out on some therapist's couch, mumbling about her childhood? No! No! Never!

She had scratched and fought to make it this far in life by herself, and she could damn well travel the rest of the road alone, too!

This new venture had to work. No one, not even her agent had to impress that fact upon her. She couldn't stand the pace of being on the road doing concerts and making recordings three weeks out of the month, then home to an empty apartment for one week. Besides, that small place she called home looked like anyone could have lived there for all the personality it held. After Noah had left her, she had fallen apart and almost ruined what career she still had. Then, after barely pulling herself together, she had spent four of the most hectic years of her life...on the road. No. She needed this new career. She needed to prove, both to herself and to others, that she was capable of acting. And she needed roots. Sometimes it felt as if she had been running all her life. She was without roots to hold her down and make her feel as if she belonged. A new career in the movies would give her those roots. She could stay in one place and never have to hit the road again. Well, almost never. Although she would have to do publicity tours, they would be shorter and not half as often. There wouldn't be any more of those lonely nights in a hundred different cities.

Reaching into her purse, she extracted her credit card,

waved to the waitress and waited for the bill. She had run in fear all her life, and now was no exception. She wasn't going to cower in some corner like a scared mouse. She wasn't!

Before long she was behind the wheel of her rented BMW and on the canyon road to the house she was to call home for the next six months. Better to be there in the afternoon and watch the sunset, than to enter in the dark and not know who or what lurked in the corners of the rooms. Or in the corners of her mind.

The road was steep in spots, twisting and turning. The BMW handled it competently, and slowly Catherine felt as if she were in control again. She passed several entrances to other elite homes, then turned into the driveway marked Castaways.

The house was a huge, golden-colored, two-story adobe with a sweeping veranda that ran across the front, from where she could sit and watch the glorious sunset. White wicker chairs were grouped around small wicker and glass tables, making cozy conversation areas for entertaining. The rooms inside were spacious with good, but functional, furniture placed to make those who entered feel comfortable. It was a house built for a family to live in—a family with children and happiness running through the wide, white halls.

She took out her key and unlocked the large double wooden doors, then walked in to stand in the entryway and listen for sounds. Only the hum of the air conditioner could be heard. Her backbone relaxed. Her hands were still clenched.

She took a deep breath. This was silly. She was a grown woman of twenty-six. She was too old to let childish fears rule her life.

She fixed a bologna sandwich, her favorite, munching away as she walked through the rooms. She didn't know what she was checking for until she realized that she had been unconsciously staring at each lock on the windows. They were all secure.

Finally, curling up on the couch, she allowed her eyes to close and drifted into a sleep that was polka-dotted with snatches of dreams and unspoken thoughts that made her restless. But she was too exhausted to waken.

It was dark both outside and in when she shot up from her curled position in the corner of the couch. She had heard a loud bang, she was sure of it. Her heart beat a fast-paced tattoo in her throat and her ears rang with the silence as she tried to listen for something else: another sound, footsteps, anything.

Slowly, very slowly, she leaned over and reached for her purse, fumbling with the clasp in her effort to find the small spray can of mace she carried everywhere. The gun was in her room under a ton of lingerie, where she had first put it when her agent had handed it to her. Someone else could play with guns, but not her, she'd probably shoot her foot off.

Once the mace was in the moist palm of her hand, she stood. She stepped into the large hallway, her eyes darting here and there. Her breath caught in her throat as she slowly walked toward the kitchen. She was sure the noise had come from the first level of the house.

She flipped on lights as she proceeded along the hallway, her eyes skimming every corner of each room she passed. By the time she reached the kitchen she was sure that whoever had made the noise was in there, waiting in the dark to pounce on her. They'd kill her, she knew it. Sweat dampened her brow and palms, making her skin itch.

With a trembling hand, she slowly pushed the swinging door wide. The light switch was on the wall to the left of her. Once the door was open, she flipped the light and brought the entire room into the brilliance of it. Out of the corner of her eye she saw something on the counter move, and she turned quickly, aiming the spray can in that direction.

"Stop!" she screamed, her finger pushing the button on the weapon.

Taut reflexes made the mace shoot forth even though she saw the mouse immediately. The rodent squealed, a high pitched sound that scraped her eardrums, then jumped and disappeared under the pantry door. Relief flooded Catherine's body, leaving her limp and damp. Suddenly a giggle rose to her throat. A mouse! The giggle turned into laughter and the laughter slowly dissolved into tears. She had tried to mace a tiny mouse!

The phone on the wall rang, a sharp piercing noise that still didn't quite register in her mind. It rang and rang. Finally the noise penetrated Catherine's crying, and with a great effort she straightened. It took all her energy to pull herself together enough to find her voice and answer.

"Hello?" Her voice was husky, breaking with the saltiness of her tears.

"Miss Sinclair? This is Sam Lewis. Are you all right?"

"No. Yes! I mean I'll be all right in a minute," she stammered, trying to gather her scattered composure. After taking a deep breath, she attempted to clear her throat. She was still staring at the tiny oil slick on the floor. The mace had hit its mark, but some had overshot and fallen like droplets to the tile below. Her eyes couldn't register the fact to her brain that she had really been trying to maim a mouse.

"Catherine? Talk to me! What's happened?" he demanded.

"I tried to mace a burglar, but it turned out to be a mouse in the pantry. I guess I thought he might be dangerous," she choked out with a sound that was a cross between laughter and tears, her voice almost as clouded as her story was. "But I'll be all right as soon as I check the upstairs and make sure there aren't any more mouses, or mice, running around."

"Give me your address," Sam said, his voice quiet but authoritative.

She did, enunciating slowly so that she could concentrate on the words. Her throat was still constricted, her nerves strung to breaking. But Sam Lewis was on the other end of the phone, making her feel that she wasn't alone anymore. He was her link to the real world, where menacing burglars and tiny mice didn't frighten her into an almost catatonic state.

"I'll be right there." And he hung up the phone with a definite click.

Catherine did the same, only more slowly, reluctant to lose the connection with another human. She was so alone. So very alone. And so very tired.

All her life she had been alone and fought for whatever she had gotten in the world. Now, when she was almost in reach of her goal, she was tired of fighting, of scrapping for every single toehold she had achieved. She was too tired to move from her place in the kitchen. She was almost too tired to breathe.

Think of something else, her mind told her, and she

obeyed. Help was on the way. What was his name? Oh, yes, Sam. Sam Lewis. She had entered his office expecting to find a paunchy, middle-aged man, slightly balding, with a "little lady" and "my dear" vocabulary. After all, with the exception of Thomas Hannover, every lawyer she had ever had contact with, and who had made a name for himself in the field, was that way.

But not Sam. He had been taller than she expected, perhaps an inch or two over six feet. Dark-brown hair and soft tobacco-brown eyes that touched her with a gentleness when they gazed at her. His frame was long and lean. No one would exclaim over his broad shoulders, for they weren't that broad, just average. His waist was thin, his hips trim. He looked like the type who had played basketball in school and had been branded with the nickname "stringbean." Only now, in his thirties she would guess, he had filled out. Very nicely.

But it was his eyes that had given her hope. His eyes were tender, understanding, caring. At least she thought they were until he had firmly explained that she had to see someone else, go through the agony of explanations again.

Slowly Catherine slid to the floor to sit, her back against the kitchen doorframe. Her legs were like rubber, her arms had no feeling. She was too tired to walk to a chair, too exhausted to do anything lately. She leaned her head against the wall and closed her eyes, her hand resting on her knee, the can of mace dangling from her limp fingers.

No, Sam Lewis was like all the rest of male mankind. He was taken with her beauty and talent, intrigued by her reputation, and not capable of seeing beyond that to the woman who was struggling to survive just below the surface. And it was just as well. No one saw that woman. They assumed that because she had been a mistress to a wealthy man, she must be hard, she must be without morals, she must be grasping. The public didn't want her to be lonely, in love, frightened or have a conscience. They wanted her to play the role of the other woman to the hilt, and she had obliged them, building upon that role to reach the position she was in today. She had been typecast before she had even had a choice of roles.

Oh, well...her agent was fond of saying that any publicity was good publicity.

The doorbell rang, and slowly she opened her eyes to stare at the ceiling. Sam. Sam Lewis. With great effort she pulled herself up and walked down the hall, the buzzer continuing to fill the house with its loud raucous sound.

When she opened the door, she was absently surprised at the look of deep concern on Sam's face, but too tired to think of why. Her emotions had been put in deep freeze and she was thankfully feeling nothing but exhaustion. She weaved slightly, holding on to the door for balance.

"My God, what happened to you?" His hands held her small shoulders, barely keeping her from falling. "What on earth is going on here!"

"Nothing. I'm just tired, that's all," she said as she pushed a stray lock of blond hair away from her eyes and stared up at him quizzically. "Here." She held out the mace she had been dangling from numb fingers.

Sam took it, muttering an expletive under his breath as he laid it on the hall table and turned her toward the living room. "Sit down before you fall down," he ordered gruffly and she did what she was told.

His eyes narrowed as he stared at her. "What's the matter with you? Have you taken something? Some drug?"

She smiled, but it never reached her eyes. "No, I don't 'do' drugs. I'm exhausted, that's all. I haven't slept in the past forty-eight hours."

"Why?"

She took a weary breath and with great effort began to explain. "I gave a late concert in Chicago, then boarded an early-morning flight. By the time the meeting with my agent was over, I had to go to that damn party. Then I came home and my necklace was stolen. The police didn't leave here until four in the morning. By then it was too late to sleep." Catherine closed her eyes, reciting the events of her days like a child reciting a poem in school.

Again, Sam muttered something under his breath, his eyes darting to the now visible lines of strain around her eyes and mouth. Even with them, she was perfection. The tailored, blue silk shirt she wore was the perfect foil for her sapphire-blue eyes and the blond hair that tumbled across her shoulders in delightful disarray.

Without saying another word, Sam sat down beside her on the couch. His dark-brown eyes searched her face, seeing a vulnerability there that stunned him. This was no man-eating shark. This was a woman at the end of her tether, trying to hold on for what it was worth.

"I couldn't sleep alone," she managed to whisper as she leaned back and closed her eyes again. But her hand found his and held on with a grip that surprised him. "Please don't leave me. I'm so tired."

"I won't." His gaze was drawn to the stark loneliness and depression that seemed to be etched on her face.

She opened her eyes and stared up at him. They were wide, blue and so very vulnerable. "And don't be mad at me, Sam," she whispered. She didn't even realize she had called him by his first name, like an old friend.

"I'm not." He barely got the words out before she closed her eyes again.

"Mmm." Her head touched his shoulder as she gave a deep sigh, completely relaxing.

Sam leaned back and brought her into the security of his arms so that they were both more comfortable. He was a fool for being here. He never should have called from April and Jace's house. He should have minded his own business and stayed out of hers.

He rested his head on the back of the couch and closed his eyes. He might as well relax. It looked as if he was going to be here awhile.

2

THE SUN SLATTED a line of brilliance across Catherine's face, and she stirred. There was a heavy, pressing feeling on her breast, and her back was against something firm but cushioned. With great effort she opened her eyes only to realize she was sleeping in the living room. Her body rocked forward and backward rhythmically once, testing. Instead of feeling the couch, she felt something else.... Tilting her head, she glanced behind her and gazed directly into Sam's sleeping face. He looked totally relaxed and a little boyish. His firm, full mouth had taken on a slight smile in sleep.

The numbness of slumber slowly left her body as she became aware of another, firmer pressure. Then she looked down. His broad, tanned hand was clasped to her breast. He had held her tenderly in his arms, toboggan fashion, all night.

Tears filled her eyes, but she willed them not to fall. Sam Lewis was the first man ever to spend the night with her and not try to make love. He hadn't even made a pass. He hadn't even made the effort. She discounted the hand on her breast. That was merely an unconscious action.

Not that she had slept with many men. There was only one she had given herself to. Noah. Contrary to the press's opinion, she had never had affairs, liaisons or lovers. Unless Noah was classified as a lover. He had also been her business partner and her love. But the fact that she had been constant to Noah hadn't mattered to the press. They continued to link her with every male she had ever spoken to, and frankly, at the time, she had treated it like a joke, going along with them because she had known better. It didn't matter what anyone else had thought, as long as she had known the real story. Now, suddenly, the stories bothered her.

Catherine pushed it from her mind and snuggled back into Sam's arms. She felt too nice and safe and warm to leave yet. She would get up in just a minute and make them both some breakfast. In just a minute. Her eyes closed and she relaxed against him once more.

WHEN CATHERINE OPENED her eyes again, the sun was blazing into the room, practically melting her. She sat up and pushed back her hair, glancing around.

Sam was gone.

Her shoulders slumped, her head bowed. An unknown anticipation seeped from her like air from a leaky balloon. She should have known he'd leave as quickly as possible. After all, she wasn't even a client of his. It was kind of him to stay the night with her, more kind than he would probably ever know, for her sleepless nights far outweighed the calm, restful ones.

He hadn't even said goodbye.

So what? She was a big girl and had been on her own for a long time. Almost too long. No, that wasn't true. She was smart, independent, beautiful. She didn't need any man to tell her goodbye.

"Morning." Sam stood in the doorway, a steaming mug of coffee in either hand as he watched her blue eyes grow wide with surprise. Her hand darted up to her hair, shoving it behind one ear as she stared at him, her wariness evident in her taut posture.

"Good morning," she answered huskily. "I thought you'd already left."

Sam raised one brow. "Without saying goodbye?"

Catherine shrugged, quickly looking down at the Oriental carpet that graced the white plush carpet beneath.

"I assure you, I've never left a lady without saying goodbye before, and I'm certainly not going to start now," he said dryly, walking into the room and setting the mug of hot coffee on the table in front of her.

"One never knows," she said flippantly, resorting to her woman-of-the-world act. It was a defense mechanism, much as her sharp tongue was. It kept her from being vulnerable. It kept others from being able to hurt.

"Well, this 'one' knows that I don't do that." His voice was rough, and his brown eyes, usually so soft, snapped with irritation. "I'm not looking for thanks, but I do expect courtesy."

"What kind of courtesy?" Did he expect her to be so grateful that she would go to bed with him? Not him, too. Please... not him, she prayed.

"A simple thank-you for the coffee would be a start."

"Thank you." Still she was tense, waiting to see what he would say next.

"Do you feel better?" His voice was etched with concern as he studied the muted circles under her eyes.

"Yes. Thank you, again."

"You're welcome." He smiled and his entire face lit up with a warm teasing that forced a melting of something deep inside her. She watched his expression, mesmerized. Her first thought didn't please her: he must have women crawling all over him with that sensuous, little-boy smile.

"Are you hungry?" she finally asked, clearing her throat. "I can make breakfast."

He shook his head, obviously reluctant. "No, thanks. I'm already late for the office." He hesitated before continuing, "Is there anything I can do for you before I go?"

Her coffee mug hit the table with a bang, her blue eyes suddenly shooting sparks at him. So much for prayers. "You mean like taking me to bed and relieving my 'frustrations'? Or helping me sleep? No, thanks!" She stood, hands on hips, breasts thrust out, as she breathed in shallow gulps of air. She had known it was coming. She had known! "And now I think it's time *I* said goodbye."

"Wait a minute!" Sam practically shouted, shock at her words turning his eyes almost black. "What the hell do you think I am? A sex maniac? All I asked was a simple question and you go all huffy! What on earth is the matter with you?"

"I know your type, Mr. Lewis." Her voice was filled with derision. "You think that just because you caught me at a low point you can climb in bed with me and I'll be eternally grateful for your attention. I'm supposed to be something of a 'nympho,' aren't I? Someone who has to go to bed with a man at least three times a day or I lose my equilibrium, to say nothing of my sanity. At least that's what the papers think. Why should you or any of your sex think any different?"

"You're crazy, you know that?" he exclaimed, frustration showing by his hand combing his hair in irritation. "If I had wanted to make love to you, do you think I would have held you all night and not done anything?"

"But you did!" she cried, then bit her lip.

"What did I do?" He looked genuinely surprised and puzzled.

"I woke up earlier and you were, you were holding..." She stopped, unable to tell him without looking like a fool.

"Your breast?" he finished, trying not to let a smile dimple his cheeks. He remembered waking to find his hand there, too. She had been so soft and warm and cuddly... "If it was so repugnant, why didn't you remove my hand?"

"Because you were asleep and I didn't want to waken you." Her defense was poor and she knew it. So did he.

"That makes a great deal of sense," he answered dryly before turning to stare out the window, a deep frown marring his brow.

Catherine waited a minute, then decided to ask the question that had bothered her all night. "Where do you live?"

"Why?" He kept his back to her, taking a gulp from his mug.

"I just wondered. You were here so quickly that you must live somewhere here in the canyons." She tried to keep her voice as indifferent as his was.

"I was visiting my partner and her husband. They live about five miles from here. Before I left, I decided to give you a call and make sure that everything was all right."

"I see."

"By the way." He finally turned to face her, but she

couldn't see his expression. The light shone into the room, making him a silhouette. "I threw away that mace. You sprayed a mouse with it. It died in the pantry. If it had been a man, you'd be in trouble. He'd have killed you."

"But you told me to protect myself!"

"That was before I knew you were trigger-happy," he said grimly.

"Oh, great. Now I get to stay in this house alone and wonder who's going to come steal me blind the next time! I have no mace, don't know the neighbors and have no attorney. Just great!" She stared up at the ceiling, willing away the tears her anger had brought forth.

"Did you get hold of Leo?"

"Not yet. His secretary said he was out of the office for the rest of the day."

Sam recalled Leo's latest attraction, a tall willowy redhead with her eye on his ring finger. She knew all the right games to play with a man like his friend.

"What about your agent? Can't he help you?"

"Oh, yes. He found this place for me so I could recuperate in solitude. He told me the same thing you did: I'd do just fine, and no self-respecting burglar would return to the scene of the crime. He didn't know why he felt so sure, but being a man, he's as pigheaded as you are, I suppose."

Silence filled the room as they each stared at the other, neither willing to disclose the more intimate but strained feelings that seemed to permeate the air.

"What are you doing tonight?" Sam finally asked, as he placed his half-empty mug on the table beside hers.

"Nothing."

"Will you have dinner with me?"

"Am I to be your latest charity case?"

"No. Am I yours?"

"No."

"I won't ask again," Sam finally said in the silence.

"I'll fix dinner here."

"I was asking so you could get out of the house for a while." Again a boyish smile changed his face, and she slowly relaxed.

"Getting out is something I always have to do. Cooking at home relaxes me. Will you join me?"

"Yes, I'd like that."

"About seven?" Her voice became throaty, her smile lit up her eyes. Now she had something to look forward to.

"About seven," he said, nodding his head in agreement. Suddenly, instead of looking like a sexy kitten, Catherine reminded him of a small, vulnerable child who was so sadly afraid of believing in good things like Santa Claus, the Easter Bunny... His smile slowly matched hers and both stood grinning at each other.

Reluctantly, Sam moved toward the door, reaching for his coat on the back of the chair as he did so. "See you then."

"Till then," she answered, not wanting him to leave her to the emptiness of the house. She badly wanted to continue talking to him.

A minute later he was gone.

Catherine stared out the window, deep in thought. She was crazy to continue this tentative relationship with a man she barely knew. She was especially crazy to invite him to dinner after practically spending the night with him. Would he expect more from her? She didn't know, but she'd have to cross that bridge when she came to it. All she really wanted was to recoup some of her lost energy and enjoy a little company...sans the sexual play that usually accompanied her relationships with men. It was at their instigation but she had learned the game well; she just picked up her marbles and left when the playing words became serious actions. No affairs for Catherine. She'd had one, which had broken her heart, and that was all she'd needed for a lifetime. Besides, Sam Lewis had not made one overt move toward her. Perhaps she had found a man who knew the meaning of friend...and knew that it wasn't automatically synonymous with lover.

A smile lifted her lips as she turned her thoughts to the day ahead. She had to plan a menu, do some grocery shopping and get ready for an evening of entertainment. She loved cooking, although she never had the time—or the kitchen—to do it properly very often. For the first time in a very long time, she had something besides work to look forward to.

"THAT WAS DELICIOUS." Sam sighed as he leaned back in the upholstered chair and patted his trim stomach. "Where did you learn to cook like that?"

"In New Orleans," she said with a smile, pronouncing the name as the natives did, almost all one word with a drawl in the center.

"Is that where you're from?" he asked a little too casually.

"Originally." She played with the remains of her New Orleans fish stew, wondering if he had noticed there was no wine with the meal. She decided not to ask. "Would you like coffee now?"

"Please;" he said, watching her every move as she

stood and gathered their plates, then turned toward the kitchen. She was wearing a silky, teal blue jump suit reminiscent of the forties. The pants were gathered into delicate pleats at the waist, and the sweetheart neckline was emphasized by tiny shoulder pads. She looked like a small, very fragile doll. His eyes drifted once more to her hips, so slim but so feminine.

"Thank you," she said smiling as she turned and caught his look.

"For what?"

"For not telling me what a great figure I have. For not making suggestive remarks. For admiring my outfit without fawning." And she disappeared into the kitchen.

Sam sat with a smile on his face. He hadn't *not* given a compliment intentionally. He had just been afraid of her reaction to anything he might say. But the fact was that she was very, very female. Being male meant that he was bound to observe, whether he commented on it or not.

When she walked in with the coffee, he was still smiling.

"You look like a satisfied cat," she said, chuckling.

"I feel like one. If you had a rag rug in front of a fire, I'd be curled up on it."

She chuckled again, a deep throaty sound that played on his nerves. He could feel his stomach muscles tense deliciously. He liked the sound. In fact, he could probably get addicted to it. . . .

"Tell me about yourself," he finally said, reaching for the steaming cup and stirring a teaspoon of sugar in it.

Suddenly her expression was closed, guarded. "What do you want to know? What's it like to be famous? Not very good. How did a nice girl like me get to the top of the business? The way everyone else does—I worked hard and clawed first. How many men are in my life? None of your business. Am I really as loose moraled as the newspapers write? Again, none of your business." Her voice was bitter, the sound cutting. Her eyes sparkled like blue steel.

Sam's spoon continued stirring the sugar slowly into his coffee. His eyes were on her, not changing expression. "No, I mean what were you like as a child. What were your favorite subjects in school? Were you skinny or fat as a teenager? What do you think of the Los Angeles Dodgers?" He placed his spoon with studied casualness on his saucer. "I wasn't interviewing, just making conversation."

Catherine's face turned a dull shade of pink. She couldn't keep her eyes focused on him. She glanced down at her hands, knotted on the table, then tilted her delightfully determined chin in the air and gave him the same steady stare he was giving her. "I'm sorry. I didn't understand."

"Apparently." His tone was dry. So was his throat, and it had nothing to do with her words.

Her eyes widened, catching his look and smiling in return. His eyes crinkled and laugh lines appeared around his beautifully soft brown eyes. She leaned back, suddenly more relaxed than she had been all week, all year. All her adult life.

"I was short and skinny. Everyone always thought I would be a midget. I surprised them all when I reached my full height of five foot two and a half inches."

His brows rose as if incredulous. "Five two and a *half*?" he repeated as if awed.

"That half may not mean much to you, but it was accomplished the hard way, by stretching a lot," she said indignantly, but her eyes gave her away. They were laughing.

"And what were your favorite subjects in school?"

"No fair. You answer first," she said quickly, crossing her arms on the table and leaning forward as if she couldn't wait for his revelations. The action caused her breasts to be pushed upward and he could see the deep fold of her cleavage. Her skin was silky, almost velvet looking. Her breasts were soft, yet he knew they were firm to the touch. . . .

He leaned back again, taking a sip of his coffee. Was it a pose she struck often, to flatter the male ego or was it natural? With anyone else he would have said that it was posed, but he wasn't sure with Catherine. She had been sending mixed messages ever since he had met her. She turned him on, then brushed him off.

"Well," he began, acting as if he were giving it much thought. "My favorite class was biology because Mary Lou Hanson was my partner and I could make her squeal when we dissected animals."

"And you liked to make her squeal?"

"No, I liked her to think I was macho, even though I had to swallow a lot to keep down my breakfast."

Catherine chuckled, a deep throaty sound that rasped against Sam's already jangled nerves.

"I didn't have any favorite subjects," she said with a smile, only the smile suddenly didn't seem to mean anything. It was empty and Sam could sense it.

"Not even one?"

She shook her head, her blond hair moving like molten gold as it touched her throat and shoulders.

"What school did you graduate from?" Sam's voice was soft, his eyes showing that he had guessed she'd had a difficult time at school and felt sorry for her.

Sorry! The blueness of her eyes almost turned black in anger. No one felt sorry for Catherine Sinclair! No one! "None of your damn business!"

As if she hadn't spoken, Sam calmly gave a rundown on his life. "I ran away from home when I was sixteen. At eighteen I joined the Marines. I took a GED test and earned my high-school diploma shortly after that, then began taking college courses in the service. By the time I left the service, at the grand old age of twenty-six, I had finished college. Then, after kicking around several years, I entered law school on the G.I. bill. It took me six years to complete it. Four of those six years I was lucky enough to work in April's office. After I graduated, I became her partner." His voice had been calm as he spoke, as if she had not been rude, screaming at him. "I was lucky."

Her eyes were wide, her lips vulnerable and parted. "Why are you telling me this?" she whispered.

"Because I'm proud of the fact that I had such an awful beginning and still made it," he answered. "Aren't you?"

"Proud of you?" Her lips twisted in derision. This was a new approach. Now she was supposed to be bowled over by his hard life.

"No." His voice was soft. He smiled. "Proud of you."

Her features froze. Her hands clasped her cup rigidly. "I think it's time I went to bed, Mr. Lewis. Last night was the first night I've had any sleep. I think I could use more."

Without another word, Sam stood. She followed him

out of the dining room and to the front door, her heels clicking on the parquet floor.

He turned, his expression one of amusement with a playful animal he didn't have the time to train. "Well, I hate to eat and run, but I'm being punished for my wayward ways. It was a wonderful dinner, Catherine. Thank you for inviting me."

"And thank you for staying with me last night. And for disposing of the mouse," she said stiltedly, obviously not accustomed to the proprieties.

"You're welcome."

Before she could move out of his way, Sam lowered his head and brushed his lips against hers in a searingly intimate fashion. Electricity filled the hallway, igniting something deep down in the pit of Catherine's stomach, and almost forced her to raise her hands to his shoulders to keep herself from falling. It frightened her. She jerked back, her eyes wide with disbelief at the reaction his touch had created.

Sam took a deep breath as if to say something, then changed his mind. "Goodbye, Catherine. I hope you sleep well."

But it took a long time for Catherine to fall asleep that night. She fiddled around in the kitchen, cleaned up the dinner dishes, then prepared a coffee cake for breakfast in the morning. By the time she was finished and locked up, it was past twelve.

The bathroom boasted one of the largest tubs she had ever seen. It also had the option of being used as a whirlpool. Knowing that it was another stall tactic to keep her from both the lonely bed and the old memories that always flooded her dreams, she used it anyway.

By one-thirty she was in bed, staring at the polished

brass fan attached to the ceiling. First she was hot, then cold, then hot again. Her mind was in a turmoil.

How could she react so strongly to a kiss from a man she barely knew and had nothing in common with? She refused to admit their pasts were similar: that did not make a bond in the world of tomorrows, only in the memories of yesterday. And they weren't even shared memories. She hadn't told him anything about herself that he couldn't have read in the newspapers. She had never told anyone, including Noah. What good would it have done? Noah would have probably hated her all the more for the person she really was, underneath all the looks and glamour. No. No one would ever know about her private past. It was better to be thought loose and immoral than it was to have the public know the truth. Hate she felt comfortable with, but pity was an emotion she couldn't handle.

When she finally closed her eyes, the sunrise was just peeking through the window to stain the room with a soft blur of light.

Her last thoughts were of Sam Lewis and the feeling of safety she had experienced in his arms. She might not like his prying, but she craved once more that feeling of total security. . . .

SAM REACHED HIS DUPLEX in record time. The first thing he did was open a bottle of Scotch and pour himself a stiff drink, no ice, no water. The second thing he did was gulp it down, then pour himself another.

His heartbeat finally slowed to a somewhat regular rate, and his head stopped throbbing.

He plopped on his custom-built, extra-long couch, careful not to spill the liquor in his glass. He sloughed off his shoes and wiggled his toes, focusing his eyes on the hole that conspicuously showed his big toe. He grinned.

Big-time attorney with his own practice and money to burn. And here he sits with a hole in his sock. If he hadn't been so damn tight most of his life, he would probably be able to throw them out with ease and buy another pair. But his Scottish ancestry called to him, telling him a needle and thread would cost less and last longer. He reminded himself to put the socks aside in the morning so that he could take care of it.

He took another sip of his drink and leaned his head back, closing his eyes. Immediately and unbidden was the vision of Catherine Sinclair as she had sat across the table from him. Her eyes a wide soft blue, her smile relaxed and utterly charming. It was the first time he had glimpsed the real her without her being tense and poised, as if on stage. She was beautiful, there was no doubt of that, but she was also a secret code that he couldn't seem to break. What made her tick? Why, when the world had one picture of her, did he have another? And his was the antithesis of everyone else's. Was his the distortion and everyone else's correct? He had always been a good judge of character until now.

She's a tramp, his conscience exclaimed in a loud voice. *No*, he answered. Did living with a man make her a tramp. . .? No, it made her unlucky in love. *But there were more men than the papers could count!* Not proven. Besides, where did he get off judging another person's love life? Hadn't he had a very active one himself? *Don't let that act of hers fool you! That's why she's here, to make a picture and put her acting skills to work!* But what if she wasn't acting tonight? What if she really was sweet, beautiful, sad and very, very vulnerable...?

"Damn!" he muttered, opening his eyes and standing up. It didn't matter what he thought of her because he wasn't going to see her again. A man would have to be stupid to fall purposely into a viper pit.

3

THREE DAYS WENT uneventfully by and Catherine reveled in it, never having had such peaceful solitude since she had begun her crazy career over seven years ago. And now, thanks to finishing a recording session earlier than usual and not having the movie script for another few weeks, she had all the time in the world. She slept, cleaned, sewed, cooked and even weeded in the beautiful gardens at the protest of the gardener who came twice a week to keep it properly manicured.

She woke late in the mornings, put on old jersey shorts and a large sweat shirt with torn neckline and sleeves, and did what she wanted. She hadn't touched a lipstick brush, makeup sponge or a mascara wand since the night Sam had come to dinner. She washed her hair every day, letting it dry in the sun before separating it into two sections and wrapping rubber bands around them. She wore them like children wore pigtails, and she loved it. It was cool with the hair out of her eyes and off her neck.

She purposely kept her mind off topics that bothered her. Topics such as work, recordings and Sam Lewis. She didn't want to delve too deeply into her instant and unexpected reaction to him. It was easier to try not to think of him than it was to judge his actions so far. Whenever thoughts of him crept into her head, she would remind herself that he was an enigma of a man, but he was still a man. . . .

Her agent, Tommy, called twice, checking to make sure she was all right and that she was resting. Both times he questioned if the insurance company had any information concerning her necklace. Both times she was amazed to find herself thinking that she didn't care whether they found it in a pawnshop or never found it at all. The necklace, as beautiful as it was, was part of someone else's life. It represented the life of Catherine Sinclair, not Kitty Slovak. Kitty was born in poverty, raised in decadence. In the past few days her life had grown into one of peace and solitude, cooking, cleaning and sewing. At night it was filled with old TV movies and interesting fiction that she hadn't had the time to read before.

Catherine Sinclair's life had its beginning shortly after running away from home. Not knowing where to go and only knowing that she had to leave, she wandered around until finally hitting Nashville. There she had taken a job emptying ashtrays and cleaning floors in an old rundown recording studio. Listening to every small piece of information that every professional singer was told by his manager or coach in the studio, she then adapted it, applying it to herself. She mimicked others, getting their musical style down pat before her own style was honed enough to come forth. She copied arrangements that seemed to fit her better than the singers who sang them. She had worked damn hard and still nothing had paid off. No one knocked on her ratty apartment door with a contract for her to sign.

Two years later she met Noah Weston, and everything that Catherine had done since was slanted toward climbing the ladder of success to make sure she was never poor or neglected or relegated to nothingness again. Her dreams were wrapped up in designer dresses and diamond necklaces, wealthy men as escorts and elegant parties given by the right people, which went on till all hours of the night. Since then everything in Catherine's life was measured by money and contacts.

One morning, Catherine posed the question to herself that had been lying on the back shelf of her mind all week. Which of those women was really her?

She didn't have the answer, and it frightened her.

SAM LEWIS SAT at his desk and watched his partner walk the floor in agitation. He grinned at her anger, for it was always quick to die.

"I don't want to have to entertain these movie moguls with myself as the only person not in show business! I can't cook, I don't keep house and I don't know a darn thing about making movies!"

"The days of the movie moguls are over, April. They have been since the late forties."

"Don't you believe it!" April said sharply. "They may have changed their style of clothing and even their image, but they're still there, acting like little tin gods, just as they always did."

He played with the pencil on his desk, making it stand end-on-end over and over again. "Then why don't you invite a few other people and have a small, informal cocktail party, followed by a buffet?" he asked calmly.

She stopped walking and stared at him, wonder in her bright blue eyes. "Sam, you're a genius! Great idea! I can have a bartender in for the drinks and cater a buffet and clean-up crew! Wonderful!" She plopped down in the chair across from him. "I knew I was smart when I made you a partner. You're not only great for the firm, you're great for my marriage!" Her expression suddenly became more subdued. "I'm just afraid I might do something that would make Jace feel embarrassed."

"Jace?" Sam exclaimed, dropping the pencil. Jace, her husband, was a well-known actor whom women clamored after, but the only one he'd ever had eyes for was April. They had lived together three years before taking the giant step into marriage, and Sam couldn't think of two people who had been happier to make the commitment. "Not on your life. Jace would love you if you walked the streets of L.A. at night. He'd be angry, but he'd still love you."

"Somehow, my loyal friend, I doubt it," she said with wry authority. "After all, it took him three years to get used to the fact that next to him, my best friend was you."

Sam gave an endearing grin. "Really? You said that before, but I assumed you were just teasing. I always thought he saw no competition from this end."

"Huh!" April groaned. "If you only knew!" She leaned forward. "But do you think it would work? The party I mean."

"Yes, if you got the right crowd and the right caterer," Sam mused. "You could find the right caterer from Jace's secretary. But the right crowd? I don't know . . ." he teased.

"Okay, okay. Tell me your plan, Machiavelli."

"You have three men coming for dinner, right?" At her nod he continued, "Then invite your secretary, my secretary, Jace's secretary, myself and my date. That should give them someone to talk to about their business and someone to talk to who makes sense."

April grinned. He was right. Sam was usually right, as well as usually being a dear friend. "That sounds great. Now, who's the lucky girl you're taking out this week?"

He hesitated. "I don't know if she'll accept."

"If *who* will accept? At least give me a clue, Sam!"

"Catherine Sinclair."

April's shocked expression was enough to make Sam look away.

"Who?" she said softly, leaning forward, obviously hoping she had misunderstood.

"You know, the Country and Western singer. You said you loved her last song, remember? Something about finding love in the most unlikely place. You drove me nuts humming that thing for weeks."

"I remember, but I didn't mean that you should date the woman just because she sings a great song." April stared at him, her furrowed brow showing her concern. He glanced at her, then back down to his desk. He knew what was coming, but he didn't want to hear it. Knowing April though, she wouldn't let it go so easily.

"My God, Sam, that woman is lethal if only half of what the papers print is true! She dines on genuine dragons! You aren't even an appetizer for a woman like her!"

"I said that I didn't know whether she'd accept, April. But if she does, that's who I'll bring," Sam said in a low tone, finally staring at her to make sure she understood his resistance to her criticism.

April stared back, her blue eyes troubled, before she eventually shrugged her shoulders in defeat. "All right, if that's what you want."

"It is," he said quietly, but with grim determination.

No matter how many times he told himself that Catherine was poison, he still wanted to be with her. He didn't understand it, for he had never been this way about a woman before. But Catherine . . . well, Catherine was different. She was street-wise, yet so very vulnerable. She was sophisticated, yet he sensed that it was an act. She was beautiful, yet not seeking flattery. She was a mystery. A puzzle he wanted to figure out. Perhaps after he did so, his attraction for her would disappear. . . .

Sam left the office at four so he could drive to Catherine's and ask her in person. The phone was too impersonal and that made it easy for her to turn him down. She could act over the phone, but somehow he knew that she couldn't act that well when he was standing in front of her. Her eyes, her movements would give him a clue as to what she was thinking. He could be wrong, but he didn't think so. It was a weak hunch, and the only one he had to play.

He could hardly believe his eyes when he pulled up in her driveway. Catherine—or someone who resembled her—was helping the gardener by bagging the branches he was expertly trimming from the shrubs that ran across the front of the yard, separating it from the road. She was in frayed, cut-off jeans and a torn, gray T-shirt that was emblazoned with a fast-food restaurant's logo. Her golden-blond hair shone in the sunlight and was caught up into pigtails that sat perkily over each ear. She looked as if she were a naive sixteen . . . and terribly content.

He stared in wonder. Something caught in his throat, and he realized he was more affected by this picture of her than the chic woman who had entered his office. His stomach tensed, his thighs tightened and his loins ached with an almost overwhelming want he didn't know he was capable of. It washed over him like a giant wave, leaving him weak and awed by its power.

He continued gazing at her, unable to do anything else. Catherine turned, apparently expecting to see someone else. She froze in midstride, her hand unconsciously going to one of her pigtails. Her smile slowly disappeared. Suddenly her chin came up and determination filled her expression. She was not going to be intimidated by being caught like this! He grinned, somehow knowing that most of her front was just that. . . a front.

"Hello, can I help you?" Catherine asked coolly as she leaned down to stick her head into the passenger window of his car.

"Yes, you can." Sam smiled his best smile. She didn't respond. "Sit in the car for a minute, will you?"

With obvious reluctance she opened the car door and sat on the edge of the seat.

"How's everything going? Any more break-ins?"

"None, thank you. My agent tells me that the insurance company is going to handle everything through you. Thank you. Apparently you and he were right. It must have been a one-time thing for the burglar."

"Are you enjoying your vacation?" Sam continued with the small questions, putting off the one that really mattered. He didn't want her to turn him down.

"I'm loving it." She turned her head and stared out the window at the gardener, but slowly his presence drew her eyes back to him.

They sat, turned on the seat, each looking at the other. The gardener's clippers and the sound of a far-off jet were the only noises to be heard.

Catherine swallowed. "Did you come by for something or were you in the neighborhood?"

"Both." He watched her throat move and he shifted uncomfortably in his seat.

She tilted her head, her eyes boring into his as if she were trying to read his mind. It wasn't working.

"And...?"

"My partner is having a small dinner party for some of the people her husband works with at the studio. I want you to be my date." *That's it, Sam, just jump right in so she can say "no" instantly!* His hand clenched the steering wheel tightly. It had been dumb to blurt it out like that. He should have led up to it, teased her with the fact that she could make some good contacts, meet Jace Sullivan, help her career along....

"I'd love to."

He cleared his throat, not able to look her in the eye for fear it would confirm that he hadn't heard what he thought he did. "Good. I'll pick you up around seventhirty tomorrow night. It's kind of casual. Bring a bathing suit if you want to. They'll be having dinner around the pool." His voice was rough and gravelly.

"Will you be bringing yours?"

"I keep one at their house." He grinned suddenly and stared into her blue eyes. "I'm there a lot," he said by way of explanation.

Her mouth pursed, and the wary tension was back in her eyes. He didn't know what he had said that had put her on the defensive again, but he wasn't going to let her change her mind now.

"I've got to run," he growled, sounding meaner than he had meant to. "I'll see you then. Be careful." His hand reached for the ignition key, ready to start the car as soon as she stepped out.

"All right." She was silent as she slid across the velour upholstery to stand by the door. "Thank you for the invitation," she murmured.

"Catherine?" Sam called, leaning over the seat to get closer to her.

She bent down. Their heads were close and both eyed the other's parted lips for seconds that seemed like eons. The drone of a plane overhead was the only sound in the world. "Yes?" she whispered throatily.

"Nothing. Just Catherine," he said, losing himself in the blueness of her eyes.

Slowly, ever so slowly, she leaned forward and allowed her mouth to brush his, sending liquid heat from his lips to the rest of her body. She held her breath with the wonder of that touch, that simple, casual touch. They stared again, each caught up in the chemistry between them and wondering with their eyes where it would lead. Sam seemed to know and Catherine fought that knowledge. She pulled away, breaking the spell.

"Thank you for asking me," she said again politely.

"You're welcome." He turned the ignition on. "See you then."

The purr of his car engine was soon lost in the distance. Catherine stood staring at the ghost of his car as it had sat in the driveway. What in the heavens was the matter with her? Was she so tired that her defenses were down? That was it. She needed more rest. She needed to recuperate so that she could once again build that wall around her, which had served her so well. He had just caught her in a defenseless moment. She'd call him and break the date. After all, she wasn't here to play footsie with an attorney when a new phase in her career was just beginning. In fact, that was the worst thing she could do.

No, she really needed rest and relaxation so that she'd be fit to walk into the studio and begin a new and very lucrative career. She would need all her wits about her, and that meant she couldn't spend time chasing romance around. It hadn't worked in the past. It wouldn't work now.

With that decision made, she began humming a song as she picked up her bag of clippings, anxious to finish the work that only fifteen minutes ago had seemed so enjoyable.

SAM PURPOSELY DIDN'T ANSWER the telephone when he got home. He also didn't accept any phone calls from Catherine Sinclair at his office the following day, giving his secretary the message that as long as she wasn't panicked, she wasn't to get through to him. His answering service would take care of any calls at home.

He had seen frightened women before. He'd also seen aggressive ones. But never had he seen the combination in one woman. Catherine was both. When she had accepted his offer of a date, she had done so without knowing the circumstances, the arguments that he had been prepared to make. When she had leaned in the car and touched his lips with hers, it was as if she had been drawn in by his very thoughts and had obeyed. But when she had gotten out of the car, he sensed she had been frightened of the feeling that existed like an invisible connection between them.

She wasn't alone. He was scared as hell, too.

Women had always been there for him. They were wild, sweet, wonderful and exciting, and he had appreciated every one, but not one was favored more than another. They were all equally great. Besides, normally his favorite type of woman was a long-legged brunette with sexy eyes and only a mouthful of breasts and gently swaying hips that showed up in a tight walk. The average model was perfect. That certainly didn't sound anything like the blond-haired, blue-eyed, tiny version of the abundant goddess of love that Catherine Sinclair was. So what special ingredient did she have that attracted him? He didn't know, but he meant to find out, if only to prove to himself that his radar had gone out of control on this one.

CATHERINE DOTTED HER BROWS with a light touch of brown pencil, cursing Sam under her breath as she did so. She had been reluctant to dress and ready herself for the man. She had tried to call him at least six times, and all with no success. Damn him! He was purposely keeping his distance because he knew that she wanted to cancel.

She held the pencil in midair, that thought claiming all her attention. Was she so easy for Sam to read that he had *known* she would try to back out? Were her thoughts and doubts so visible? Had she lowered her defensive wall so much that it was only rubble at her feet for him to step over?

Her face paled. No! No, no, no! She couldn't have. Not her. Not after years of building her wall so strong that no one, including Noah Weston, could climb it.

With shaking hands she lowered the pencil to the dressing table top and stared at herself in the mirror.

Her shoulders were slumped, her neck bent down so that her chin almost touched her breast. Suddenly she stood straight and tall. Her chin lifted with a determined tilt. Well, if Sam Lewis thought he could read her like a book, he had another think coming.

She'd fool him. After all, she was supposed to be an actress. How good was her acting ability if she couldn't fool one lone attorney?

She smiled, and the mirror reflected the impishness of her thoughts. Mr. Sam Lewis was going to be given a lesson in reading and interpreting the actions of others. The smile turned into a chuckle as she quickly put the finishing touches on her makeup.

By the time the doorbell rang, Catherine was ready for anything. The adrenaline ran quickly through her veins. She was rejuvenated for the first time in a long time. There was a sparkle in her eyes and a daring challenge to the tilt of her chin. She was alive!

"Why, hello, Mr. Lewis," she said gaily, opening the door wider to allow him entrance. "My, you look handsome!" Her gaze roamed appreciatively over his tall, lean form. He was wearing gray slacks with a white knit, open-collared shirt that sported an alligator on the pocket.

She touched the alligator with a long nail. "Are you sure that thing won't bite?"

"No," he answered, his brown eyes narrowing as he watched the mischief flitting across her beautiful face.

"No, it won't bite, or no, you're not sure?" she teased as she walked to the bar and held up a bottle of wine, silently asking him if he cared for some. He nodded, his brows still drawn together in a frown that told her of his confusion. A giggle rose in her throat, but she swallowed it down as she turned her back and poured him a drink. Then carefully, she picked up her own, a long-stemmed glass of lemon water. It looked for the world like white wine.

"Are you feeling all right?" Sam asked, his voice low, his concern showing in the golden light of his dark-brown eyes. "Is everything going well?"

Catherine turned, that impish smile back on her lips. "I'm fine, better than ever. Everything's going very well, thank you."

"My secretary said that you called several times. I'm sorry I couldn't get in touch with you, but there were some extenuating circumstances. . . ." He let his voice drift off, expecting her to fill in with her answer.

"Oh, think nothing of it," Catherine said with a grin. "You had told me to dress casual, but you didn't give specifics. I was just worried about what to wear and thought you might know. But—" she shrugged "—since I couldn't ask you, I just decided to wear what I had and not worry about it."

"That was all?" His brows rose in wary disbelief. Her outfit was stunning as well as being perfect for the informal California occasion. A pure white harem jump suit, the front yoke was latticed to give a peek at the deep cleavage of her breasts, while the thin spaghetti straps barely seemed to hold the lightweight, gauzy material up. It was a striking, very sensuous outfit as well as being almost virginal in appearance. The woman was full of contradictions.

She nodded, sipping on her chilled drink. "That was it," she said breezily. The giggle began to form again at his doubting but confused expression, and she took another sip until it passed.

Sam placed his glass back on the bar and turned toward the door, his irritation barely kept in check. "Are you ready? We don't want to be late," he said, leading the way to his car.

Quickly she placed her glass on the table and grabbed her purse, her small legs working twice as hard to keep up with his long ones.

When they reached the bottom step of the front garden, she stopped. Sam was around the front of the car before he noticed her standing there.

"What's the matter?"

"I'm waiting for my escort to do just that: escort me from my house to the car door. It's usually the gentlemanly thing to do, isn't it?"

His stiffened shoulders slowly relaxed, his frown turned into a small, rueful smile. He walked toward her, stopping only when he was almost touching her. Their heads were level, their lips a tiny space apart. His hand reached for and grasped hers, holding it in the warmth of his. "I'm being rude, aren't I?"

Catherine nodded, suddenly feeling breathless and unexpectedly excited at his nearness.

"And you're being sweet and charming."

Catherine shook her head at that statement. Once more a smile formed around her mouth and she chuckled. "No, I was being a real stinker, only you didn't recognize it." She tilted her head to the side and stared at him. "Are you always so trusting of a female's attitude?"

It was his turn to chuckle. "Not normally, but ever since I met you, I've had a hard time fitting you into the mold of the 'usual female.'"

Anyone else could have said those words to her and

she would have brushed them off. But when Sam said them, she felt flattered. "Why?"

"Because you aren't."

"Why?"

"You're one of the few women I know who plays at being self-sufficient and is really sweet and vulnerable. Most women do it the other way around," he said huskily, staring into the blue of her eyes while trying to control the almost overwhelming urge to kiss her senseless.

"Sam?" she whispered.

"Uh-huh?" he answered. His eyes darted down to her lips, staring at the sweetness of her mouth as she formed his name.

"If you don't kiss me, I think I'm going to have to kiss you."

"Go ahead, beautiful."

She took her hand out of his and placed both hands on his tall shoulders. With infinite care, she stood on tiptoe and very carefully, almost shakily, touched his mouth with hers. The contact was electrical.

Sam stiffened, then his arms moved quickly, wrapping around her small waist and back, almost crushing her to him as he made their contact more intimate. Every emotion she had ever felt was buried under a mountain of exploding need. Her mind froze, and only the heat of his lips and hands were allowed to give fire, the rest of her was numb. A low moan surfaced from his throat as he parted her lips with an urgency he hadn't known he was capable of and took the honey of her mouth with his darting tongue.

Her hands slid from his shoulders to the back of his neck, pulling him ever closer in a crazy, whirling moment of sheer madness. Her head spun from his touch, her body felt alive and shouting with needs that had to be met and satisfied. She absorbed the hard leanness of his chest and ribs, the heavy fabric of his slacks as she pressed against him to imprint his maleness on her abdomen and revel in that feeling. She moved, side to side, and another moan echoed between them, but she didn't know from whom.

His grip on her didn't lessen as his lips left hers to travel from her mouth to her cheek, finally to rest by the side of her ear. "My God!" he whispered, almost to himself, in awe of the intensity of feelings they had just created by merely touching.

Catherine closed her eyes and tried to control her wildly beating heart. "Ditto," she murmured shakily, hoping there was a small sound of laughter in her voice so that he wouldn't know just how traumatic his kiss had been.

Slowly, she pulled away. Where was her wall of defenses she had worked so hard at building? Where was her cool reserve that froze most men out? Where was her fierce pride and self-sufficiency? And why this man? Her mind kept churning with questions, but for the life of her she couldn't have come up with the answers. Her brain seemed to be in a chaotic state even as she tried to retain a measure of her usual thought processes. It didn't work. She was stunned.

Pulling away from Sam's touch was one of the hardest things she'd ever had to do, but she finally summoned enough energy to accomplish it. She turned, head down, and walked slowly toward the car.

Sam stood where he was, his head turned to watch her. "Catherine?"

When she reached the car door, she looked at him, her brows raised, her nose pinched with the effort. "Yes?" Her voice was tight, her face barren of expression.

"Nothing," he snapped. "Just Catherine." And with that he joined her, opening the door and allowing her entrance before walking around to his side and seating himself as close to the door as was humanly possible and still be able to drive.

The engine roared to life and they pulled down the drive in silence.

Catherine sat rigid in her seat. She had asked for that kiss. She was stupid enough to have *asked*.

Then she had responded as if she had been starving for love. Her only consolation was that he had been as shaken as she was. It was going to be a tension-filled evening. . . .

She'd ignore the entire situation tonight, making sure that Sam realized he had no hold on her. That would put him in his place. Then, after tomorrow, she vowed silently, she'd never see him again. Sam Lewis, for whatever reason, was too volatile for her system.

CATHERINE WAS AFRAID to admit that with each mile the car ate she was becoming more nervous of meeting his friends. She had never been the type to have friends—acquaintances and business contacts, yes. But hardly ever friends.

They pulled into the driveway, and she tried to concentrate on the massive, one-story hacienda before her, but all it did was increase her tension.

She didn't do well with women. She never had. She didn't even know why. She should have stayed home, rejecting Sam at the door rather than let her sense of pride get in the way. Perhaps she should invent some excuse.

Sam killed the engine and reached for her clenched hands. "You'll like April," he said softly, as if he knew what she was thinking.

"I'm sure I will." Her eyes widened as she painted a smile on her face. With a deep breath she realized that it was too late to do anything but brazen it out. One miserable evening wasn't going to kill her as long as she didn't think about all the other miserable evenings she had regretted.

Before Sam could reach for the doorbell, the door was opened. "Hi! Come on in!" April said cheerily, waving Catherine and Sam through the entrance and into the large tiled hall. The dark-haired woman's white, frilly apron was slightly askew, her finely boned face filled with obvious delight at seeing her partner. "Since you're the first ones here, I can put you two to work. Jace is in the wine cellar, deciding what goes with anything burned."

"Wine cellar?" Catherine murmured, glancing around. It was a big, sprawling, contemporary house, but didn't seem the type to sport such a prestigious item as that.

April chuckled. "A temperature-controlled closet actually, but it sounds so much better the other way. Especially when I'm trying so hard to impress someone."

Sam sniffed the air. "Anything burned? I thought I advised you to get a caterer, April. Jace may like your burnt offerings, but think of the rest of us who haven't cultivated a palate for your efforts!" Sam glowered at the lovely girl who was supposed to be old enough to be his law partner. His hands were on his hips, his face wore an angry scowl. At first Catherine was afraid he had lost his temper and a bolt of fear ran down her spine. Then she noticed the beginnings of a smile denting his mouth.

April reached up to plant a careless kiss on his cheek, not at all put off by his cold glare. "I did, Sam. I did. But I decided I wanted to make the hors d'oeuvres. What Jace doesn't know is that they're grapes, cheeses and crackers. Just to teach him a lesson, I burned some butter on the stove. He thinks I'm burning stuffed mushrooms!" Her giggle was infectious.

Catherine watched the banter only two good friends could participate in and felt more alone than she had in a long time. It was so obvious that they were good friends with a wealth of small, private jokes between them. Why else would they laugh at burned butter?

"Don't you think so, Catherine?" April said, turning to her.

"I'm sorry?" Catherine started, her mind once more coming back to the present. Her brows rose haughtily as she tried to put distance between herself and the other woman. Never make friends, especially with women, was her motto.

"I said I thought the least Sam could do is act as bartender until the real McCoy got here. After all, friends are supposed to help out. Right?"

"Are you sure? Knowing the only mixed drink I can make with complete accuracy are deadly margaritas?" His hand touched Catherine's arm as he slowly, but purposefully, led her into the large, bright living room. Her skin tingled as they walked across the carpet to the impromptu bar set in the corner.

"Ugh." April's voice showed her opinion of his specialty. "Just do the best you can."

"Right," Sam said. "I know what April wants to drink, but what will you have, Catherine? White wine?"

"A fruit drink, please," she said stiffly. Sam raised his brows but he did her bidding.

The moment she reached the end of the room, Catherine turned and took a few steps away from Sam's side. It was hard enough to be in the same room with him, let alone so near him. The air around him sizzled with electricity. He was too potent for her to feel completely relaxed.

April continued her teasing, and Sam countered by making fun of her apron, the only sign of domesticity he had ever seen her in. Catherine smiled as they chuckled, her mind already separating from them to dwell in her own quiet world. It didn't pay to get close to people. It was too risky.

A loud crash, cursing and a yell brought Catherine back to the present with a thud.

"Damn! April! Where's the broom?" A voice boomed through the house. "I broke my best bottle of cheap wine, thanks to that blasted tabby cat you rescued from a very deserved death!"

April's eyes widened knowingly as she turned to Catherine. "Excuse me, won't you? My lord and master has just had another major battle with the cat...and lost again!" she said with a giggle.

As soon as April rounded the corner toward the back of the house, the smile was gone from Sam's eyes. "What's the matter, Catherine?" he asked, his eyes searching hers. She stared back, almost daring him to be nice.

"Not a thing. Why? Aren't I friendly enough for your friends?"

"You won't hurt my friends' feelings, only mine. Now, what's the matter? Don't you like April?"

She evaded the answer by changing the subject. "Why would someone purposely burn butter?"

"Because that 'someone' can't cook worth beans. She and Jace eat out or order out most of the time. She just doesn't have the knack, and Jace is always afraid she might try. It's become a joke between them." He gazed down at her. "But that still doesn't answer my question. Don't you like her?"

"She's very nice," Catherine replied stiffly, wishing she had obeyed her first instinct and not come at all.

"I'm just not much into gossip and banter and women's talk, that's all."

"Neither is April."

"Really? She does a good job for not liking it." Catherine turned toward the window and stared unseeingly at the vista before her. Her spine was rigid, her head tilted determinedly. He was *not* going to get through to her. He hadn't given her the right to turn down this invitation, so he could just suffer the consequences. The tiny fact that she had decided to pretend that she wanted to come was ignored. After all, being female meant that she had the right to change her mind!

"Catherine, look...I..." Sam ran a hand through his hair, obviously puzzled by her reaction. How many faces did Catherine Sinclair have?

She held up her hand, turning to stave off his questions. "Please, let's just leave this for a better time?" She nodded toward the hallway. "Your, uh, friends are returning."

It was with great effort that Sam held his tongue, and Catherine almost smiled as she watched his face draw into thin lines of resignation. If Sam found her easy to read, it was at least a two-way street.

"Sam!" Jace boomed from the doorway, his hand extended as he took giant strides across the room. He was dark-haired and dark-eyed, and as handsome as any movie sex symbol could be. His face was lined in a smile as he entered the room, not seeing Catherine or her open-mouthed stare. "It's a good thing you're here. Maybe you can tell my wife that she shouldn't be allowed anywhere near the kitchen unless she's pouring a glass of water!"

"Jace?" Catherine whispered throatily. "Jace Sullivan? Is that you?" With a glad cry, she hurled herself into his arms, laughing and crying at the same time.

Jace's initial reaction was one of shock, until he took a good look at the blond bundle in his arms. "Kitty? Kitty!" he exclaimed, a deep, bounding chuckle resounding through the room. "Well, I'll be damned! How on earth did you get here?"

Her infectious laughter filled the room as he gave her another hug. "Sam brought me. I'm out here to do a remake of *Oklahoma*. But you! Who would have ever thought I'd find you! And domesticated! My, how the mighty have fallen!" she teased.

"Apparently I wasn't that mighty," he said with a laugh, holding her away from him to get a better look. "Either that, or the state of grace I'm in because I found April means that I can't fall...or fail. And you? Are you still the single, swinging bachelorette that you promised you'd be?"

"Oh, yes. When I make a solemn promise, I keep it! Too bad I can't say the same for you!" she quipped, pulling out of his arms. She gave his hands a squeeze and stared up at him as if he were still an apparition.

"I've followed your career. Congratulations. You did it, babe, and all by yourself." Jace's eyes were filled with admiration.

Sam cleared his throat to speak, but April beat him to it. "Would either of you care to explain yourselves before I hit both of you with the first thing available? After all, I'm the wife of the mightily fallen man and Sam is the high-flyer's date."

Both Jace and Catherine looked surprised at the sudden interruption in their conversation. Then they glanced at the other two before breaking out in giggles.

"It's simple really, darling," Jace began. "I met Kitty six years ago in Nashville when I was doing one of those low budget movies we don't talk about. I was low, she was low, and we became friends. We made lots of promises to each other over drinks, most of which we promptly forgot, except for the career choices. After I left Nashville, we kept in touch for a while, but then..." He shrugged, as if that explained it all.

Apparently it didn't, for Catherine could sense more seeds of doubt had been planted in April's mind.

She smiled. "Please, there was never anything but a friendship between two people on the bottom rung of the career ladders. We didn't even hold hands."

Jace's eyes glittered with laughter. "Well, there was that hot and steamy kiss we shared when you took me to the airport," he drawled teasingly, only to have Catherine hit him solidly on the shoulder.

"Stop that, Jace! You know better. That kiss was on the cheek and as chaste as they come. The closest you ever got to me was calling me 'Kitty' when you knew I hated that nickname! Don't you tease your wife so, especially with me. Don't I get enough of that from the press as it is?"

"You're right, I'm sorry." Jace tried to look repentant, but the gleam was still in his eye as he glanced at his wife. "But at least it will be a week or so before April calls me a big lug again. She has a tendency to deflate my ego."

"And you definitely need it!" April stated emphatically, but a relieved smile was pulling at her mouth just the same. She got a glimpse of Sam's face as he placed his drink on the bar. She believed them, but Sam didn't, if his frown was anything to go by. "Well, Catherine, again . . . welcome to our home. Jace has spoken of a Kitty but he never mentioned last names." She took Catherine's hand in hers and gave a light squeeze. "I'm glad you're here," she said sincerely.

For no reason that Catherine could fathom, tears glistened in her eyes and she nodded her head before turning away to reach for her drink. She didn't see Sam's cautious look or Jace's comforting wink to his wife.

"Thank you. I'm glad I came, too. I met Jace at a low point in my life and, like a good friend, he helped me through it. It's nice to know that he found the happiness he deserved."

It was the most touching and honest thing Sam had ever heard her say about another person, and again he was surprised. What kind of woman could change so rapidly from one personality to another? A witch? Perhaps. He slowly let out his breath and tried to will away the jealousy that had risen within him. Catherine wasn't his and he had no right to that emotion. *Calm down, man,* he told himself, but his muscles weren't listening. They were still knotted. This was crazy. He wanted to throw her over his shoulder and storm out of the door and into his car, driving her as fast and far away as possible from Jace Sullivan. He took another deep breath and let it out in a sigh, not bothering to listen to the teasing conversation around him. This was definitely going to be a long evening, so he'd better pull himself together.

THE PARTY WAS A HUGE SUCCESS if the easygoing laughter of the guests was anything to go by. Sam sat and watched the interplay between Catherine and all of the men, astounded that she was so relaxed. Only a few times had she tensed up, but Jace had been there and had intervened between her and one of the producers, named Lenny. He had obviously read a lot about Catherine and truly believed the printed word. But before Sam could come to her rescue, Jace had been there, turning the innuendo into a harmless joke and once more things had died down. Everything except the look that Lenny occasionally cast in Catherine's direction. From that point on, Sam hadn't left her side.

She didn't seem to mind his being close, but she didn't seem to care, either. Damn her! Couldn't she see she was tying him in knots?

Once or twice Catherine had helped April in the kitchen. It was a good thing, because April would have burned the dinner if she had been given a chance to warm the meal that the caterer had left. For April everything was either on high or off. She didn't seem to know there was an in-between.

Sam was sure the food wasn't really sawdust, but he was hard pressed to taste anything, so intent was he on taking care of Catherine before Jace could. Why couldn't Jace be a stranger? How could anyone just be a friend to Catherine?

Finally the evening came to an end, and the guests began drifting into the night until only Sam and Catherine were left.

Jace closed the door and returned to the living room, a big smile on his face. "Well, how about a midnight swim?"

Catherine and April both grinned conspiratorially at his boyish charm. "No, thanks, Jace." Catherine sighed regretfully as she stood and stretched. "I'm for bed. I'm supposed to be resting up."

"Party pooper," April teased, but her eyes were on Jace.

"In that case, it's time to go." Sam rose stiffly, his face stern as he possessively reached for Catherine's hand to lead her out to the car.

"Where are you staying, Kitty?" Jace asked, his glance taking in Sam's proprietary hold. He barely contained his grin. So old Sam was smitten at last.

"At Jimmy Reingold's house, about five miles from here," Sam said stiffly.

"The one with the sign that says Castaways?" Jace prodded much to Sam's annoyance.

April didn't seem to notice his goading. "And I already have the number," she chimed in, her face smiling as she gave Catherine's shoulders a light squeeze. "We won't lose her this time."

Catherine barely held back the lump of feelings that had lodged in her throat. "Thank you," she said softly, her blue eyes looking into April's as if to indicate some things were best left unsaid.

"You're welcome," April said gently.

Unspoken communication seemed to flow between the two women. Finally Sam coughed to gain their attention.

"Ready?" he said gruffly, and she nodded before giving Jace a peck on the cheek.

Her blue eyes glinted mischievously. "Take care, Jace."

"You bet I will." Jace's arm spanned the back of April's waist, giving a squeeze. "Finding gold at ends of rainbows usually isn't my style, but I'm not dumb enough to lose it once I have it."

The ride home was silent. Catherine's head rested on the back of the seat, a small smile parenthesizing her mouth.

Sam's fingers tightened on the steering wheel, his eyes straight ahead as he drove the winding road through the canyons. Before he could think of something clever to say or witty to throw out as bait for a conversation, they were there. He turned into the drive and pulled as far up as he could, flipping off the lights with a controlled, angry action before swiveling in his seat to confront Catherine. Somehow she must have known that he wouldn't let her go yet, for she was sitting perfectly still, her eyes staring out the windshield, her hands clasped loosely in her lap.

Without volition, Sam's hand reverently touched the spun gold of her hair, sliding it between his fingers. He was almost caressing it, watching it change color as he moved it from shadow to light. A golden girl—all white and gold and so very sweet smelling. She was so very beautiful and so very far away. . . .

"Did you love him?" Sam finally asked in a low and rasping tone. Visions of Jace and Catherine marched in his head.

"I thought so. Very much," Catherine said slowly, her voice seeping into his brain to make the pain even more sharp. Noah's face drifted in front of her.

His hand hesitated only a moment before continuing to play with her hair. "Did he love you?"

"Looking back? No." Her voice tightened and she swallowed. "I don't think he ever did, even though I wished it with all my heart. I guess I thought my wishing would make it come true."

"The bastard," Sam muttered under his breath, wondering how anyone could not love her. He was also wondering how he could get away with punching Jace's face in.

"No." Catherine gave a small sad smile in the darkened interior of the car. "I was just silly for trying to make myself believe something that I unconsciously knew was false. I only believed what I wanted to believe. It wasn't his fault. He didn't lead me on." And he hadn't. Noah had told her from the beginning that he only wanted "companionship" from her. She was the one who had hoped, even dreamed, to change his mind.

Sam wrapped a small curl around his index finger. "How could he not care?" He said it almost casually, as if discussing the weather.

"He cared. But I wasn't asking for care," she said, a small note of sadness tinging her voice. "I was asking for love."

"Okay, then how could he not love you?"

Slowly, very slowly, her head turned, her large blue eyes straining in the semidarkness to see into his. An expression of disbelief was on her face. "Do you love me, Sam?"

He hesitated, lost in the midnight-blue spell of her eyes. Finally he answered. "I don't know."

She smiled then, a big beautiful smile that he felt all the way down to his Topsider shoes. His breath caught in his throat. His heart hammered out the real answer in Morse code.

Catherine leaned forward. "Good. Don't." Her lips suddenly brushed his, as if in passing, but the electricity that he had felt before was still there and ready to leap between them.

Before he could make it a more lasting kiss, she was

out of the car and walking toward the front door, giving a jaunty wave over her shoulder.

Sam sat in his seat watching the musical movements of her body as she climbed the steps to the veranda. She was charming, witty, sweet, vulnerable and famous. And she was in love with Jace.

His stomach clenched and he almost wanted to throw up at that last thought. Bile rose in his throat at the injustice of it. He wanted her. God, but he wanted her! And that want would get him exactly nothing.

As Catherine slipped the key into the lock, Sam turned on the ignition in the car.

As she stepped in the door, he slammed the car in reverse.

As the lights went on, he carelessly backed his way down the dark drive, his head turned so that he could follow the general curve of the concrete.

As she flew down the driveway toward him, he spun the car around to head in the direction he was going.

Suddenly he stopped.

As she flew down the driveway! His thoughts froze as he watched her racing toward him. Blood pounded in his head as he realized the terror that was making her feet have wings. He could see the expression of stark fear on her face. As she got closer, he could see the tears running down her cheeks, he could hear the sobs that threatened to escape loudly into the night air.

He slammed the car into park, pulled the emergency brake and jumped from the car, racing toward her. They met at the end of the driveway. She crumbled into the shelter of his arms, almost knocking him down with the impact.

Her words were barely coherent. "He's been there,

Sam! He came back! I think he's still there! The house!
Oh, my God, the house!"

"Wait a minute!" Sam exclaimed. "Tell me again.
What happened?" He held her head in his hands, his
eyes searching for the answers before her mouth could
form the words. But all he saw was stark fear, a terror
that she felt so deep her skin was frozen with it.

"Someone's in the house. At least I think he's still
there. The living room is torn apart, pillows messed, the
TV's gone, the stereo's gone. I don't know what else!"
She grabbed the front of his shirt, her eyes pleading.
"Don't you understand? He came back! The burglar
came back!"

"Shhhhh," Sam said, his mind working as quickly as
greased lightning. "Don't worry. You're safe."

"Safe?" she cried, hiccuping as she angrily swiped at
the tears on her cheeks. "Why? Just because you're here?
You were in the driveway when I walked into the house!
I was unprotected!"

"I know, but I'm with you now!" Sam shouted, just as
angrily. "You're the one who can do without macho
men around, playing games you think always lead to
sex! If I had insisted and walked you to the door, you
would have thought I was after your body!"

Her eyes grew wider, her tears stopping. "Weren't
you?"

"Yes, dammit!"

The sound of a distant car engine grew to a dull roar,
and a vehicle came veering around the bend of the hill.

"Oh, no!" Sam exclaimed, pulling her along after him
as he made a gesture for the driver to slow down and go
around his car. Brakes screeched and the car turned,
missing the bumper of Sam's car by inches.

"Get in!" he yelled, shoving her toward the passenger side of his car before running around to the driver's side. Once more, he slammed the car in gear and began driving down the hill.

Catherine sat huddled in the corner of the seat, her legs and arms trembling as if she had caught a chill. Her teeth chattered in the silence, punctuated only by Sam's murmured cursing as he negotiated each curve.

They were at Jace's house in ten minutes. Grabbing her arm, Sam led her to the front door and began pounding, his anger apparent in every gesture.

"What the..." Jace stood in the doorway, his hair rumpled, feet bare, and a pair of jeans hastily donned, if their unbuttoned state was anything to go by. Despite her fear, Catherine had to smile.

Sam brushed by Jace, continuing to hold her arm in a viselike grip until they got to the center of the hallway.

"Someone broke into Catherine's house. I've got to call the police," was his terse explanation as he walked toward the hall telephone.

"When?" Jace was alert now.

"Just now."

"Did they take anything?"

"Stereo, TV, maybe more. I don't know." Sam punched out the numbers and waited, his expression set in stone as he sent a narrow-eyed look in Catherine's direction.

"Are they still there?"

"Don't know," Sam said again. Then he began talking to the officer on duty, and Jace walked over to Catherine, putting his arms around her. She clung to him, finally letting go of the panic as she realized she was really safe. Tears began again and she softly sobbed into his chest.

Her eyes ached, her back ached, her neck ached. She didn't know when April walked in with a shot glass of whiskey; she only did what they told her and drank it straight down, not even wincing as it burned her throat.

April was saying something to her as she sat on the couch, but all she could do was nod her head, mumbling yes or no. She was frozen inside, as if someone had poured ice cubes into her system. It was silly to have such a strong reaction. She was a very capable woman, why wasn't she behaving like one? Why couldn't she stop this shivering? It was as if her mind was working on two different levels: one was logical and responsive, the other was somersaulting in sheer panic.

Sam leaned down in front of her, his face level with hers. "Catherine? I'll be back in a while. I'm going to meet the police at your house. We'll get to the bottom of this."

Her hand reached out to touch and slide across the side of his strong jaw, feeling the beard that was forming. "Sam," she murmured, tears filling her eyes. "Don't. Let the police handle it. Please?" Somehow, even as she said the words, she knew that he would go.

He stood and her hand trailed back to lay lax in her lap. Without another word, he left. And a part of her heart went with him.

APRIL MADE FRESH COFFEE laced with brandy and the three of them, April, Jace and Catherine, sat in a tightly knit circle at the kitchen table and waited in tense silence. Jace asked her once more what happened, and this time she was able to give him a fairly capable account of it.

She told him of the mess in both the hall and living room. What she couldn't express was the fear of the unknown person in her home, violating her privacy, perhaps hurting her. . . .

The minutes slowly ticked by on the wall clock.

Catherine's thoughts turned to Sam. Sweet Sam. She surprised herself with that notion. After her misspent youth and then Noah Weston, she thought she'd never think of a man as being sweet again. Oh, not that Sam wasn't also contrary, abrupt and panting after her like all the others. But there was something very different about him. His anger tonight had frightened her for a moment. It had scared her enough to forget about her own plight and worry about his, until she realized that even in a temper he would never hurt her.

She almost chuckled to herself when she remembered his admission about wanting her. He had practically shouted it from the rooftops! And he had looked so very, very frustrated!

And suddenly she knew. All the signs were there: the electricity between them; her wanting to continue to touch him and forcing herself to leave distance between them; even her own mind connection with him.

She cared for Sam Lewis more than she had ever dreamed possible.

But why? Certainly it wasn't because of his long lean looks, or his sexy bedroom eyes. It wasn't because he was an attorney who made a great deal of money. After all, she had more than plenty of that commodity herself. Was it because he was witty, fun to be with, seeming to know what was on her mind before she did? Was it because he was so honest in his answers and expected her honesty, too?

She did not have the answer, and that frightened her more than the burglar's visit had. Sam's narrow-eyed look when he left told her that he was angry with her again. But why? Perhaps if she had told him of her fears.... No. She'd never tell anyone. Not anyone.

Damn! All she knew was that she wanted to be in Sam's arms. She wanted his reassurance that everything was going to be okay. She wanted his lips on hers, his hands touching her. Now.

Two hours later she had run through all the things she should have said to Sam. She was also very tipsy and wide awake. April had refilled her coffee with brandy at least five times, and she had never objected. She had never said, no thank you, as she usually did, nor did she reject drinking the brew.

Jace had been on the phone several times, but the wordless messages had passed between him and April, leaving Catherine out of it. She would glance up and see the looks in their eyes, then, without bothering to figure out their silent code, she would stare out the window again. She didn't care. If there wasn't news of Sam, she wasn't interested.

Her shaking had stopped long ago, but with each passing minute now, it was returning. Her legs, her hands, even her arms were quaking as if she were chilled from the night air. It was nothing but fear, she kept telling herself as she tried to calm down. Only this time her fear was for Sam's safety. Where was he?

Wherever he was, when he returned she was drunkenly determined to give him a hero's welcome. He deserved it for being there when she needed him most. Yes, her fuzzy mind proclaimed, a hero's welcome was just what was needed here.

Just as soon as the damned hero turned up!

5

A SCREECH OF TIRES in the driveway brought April and Catherine's heads swiveling toward the front door. Jace got up from the couch and stood facing the entryway, his face a mask of suppressed feelings as he waited for Sam to walk in.

Questions ran around in Catherine's mind like small darting fish. Had they caught the burglar? Who was he? Or was it a she? A shiver of apprehension slithered down her spine. The brandy was making her body lethargic but her mind was still traveling too quickly for her to understand fully.

The door opened and Sam's lean, hard body filled the frame. His brown hair was mussed disarmingly, falling in a wave over his forehead. His clothing was still neat and casual, but his shoes were caked with a rim of dark mud. His gaze locked with Catherine's, noting the light touch of pink in her cheeks from the liquor she had drunk.

Catherine slowly stood, as if waiting for a sentence from a judge. Her knees shook with reaction. "Sam?" she croaked and his shoulders loosened at her words. He was all right. That was all that mattered. To hell with the house. Sam was safe.

His dark-brown eyes bored into hers, intense and calming at the same time. Slowly she relaxed, but her eyes continued to watch his every move. There was a muscle twitching on the side of his jaw showing her just how tense he was.

"We didn't find anyone, Catherine," he said in a low voice. "But the police are still there, looking for more clues."

"Does that mean they've found some?" Jace questioned, and Sam's eyes darted to his before focusing back on Catherine.

"Too many. They thought they had his footprints, only to find the gardener's boots in the greenhouse. The flowerbeds are full of tracks now, it's hard to say which are the gardener's and which belong to the police." His voice was low and his frustration was evident.

Jace raised his brows then reached across Catherine to hold his hand out to April. "Let's make some tea or coffee or something," he said quietly, walking his wife out of the living room.

Catherine barely noticed Jace and April leaving. She had been concentrating solely on Sam since he walked in the door. But only when he was directly in front of her and his arms wound around her still-shaking form to enclose her in his warmth did she feel safe. But not safe enough to stop the trembling of her mouth and the tears from clouding her eyes. Her arms wrapped around his waist as if fearful of letting go and losing him.

"You saw?" she murmured into his shirt front.

"Yes," he answered grimly. "I saw." His hand stroked her cap of golden hair, his cheek rested against the top of her head.

"It was awful," she said with a shudder. "Those things . . . those vicious words written on the hall mirror." She choked back the sob that threatened to explode in her throat.

"Who did it, Catherine?" His voice was so low and soothing and tender that she almost missed the import of his words.

Her throat tightened even more. "I don't know."

"Yes, you do. There was more of the same scrawled on the mirrors and windows all over the upstairs. Only someone who knew you could have written those things. Someone who wanted to hurt you deeply. Who do you think it was?" Her face was still burrowed in his shirt, his hands still stroked her hair. Only the tension had changed.

When Sam had first walked in she had felt the invisible, but tangible, tension that always seemed to be between them. Now, with his words, the tension was all transferred to the inside of her, acting like a tightly wound rubber band around her stomach.

He leaned back, taking in the whiteness of her face, the tension that drew her mouth into a small "o." Her eyes looked like dark pools surrounded by stark white sand. "Who was it, Catherine?"

She slowly moved her head back and forth, denying any knowledge even before she could say the words. "I don't know." It was easy to twist out of his arms and walk across the room to the dark windows. Her hands stroked her upper arms as if warding off a chill. "I didn't see the upstairs, remember? I just walked in the door, saw the mirror in the hall and the mess in the living room."

Sam heaved a heavy sigh. "Catherine, please tell me what you know, or what you might suspect. I can't help you if I don't know what I'm looking for."

"I don't know who would do such a thing, either." Her voice was tight, strung wire-thin with tension.

"Yes, you do," he persisted quietly.

She whirled around. "No!"

"Why would someone hate you so much they would write on mirrors that you're a husband stealer and a slut?" His voice was almost conversational in tone. "Who would hate you so much that they would take the time to do that instead of just robbing you?"

Panic started at her toes and threaded its way up her body. Her hands clenched as if ready to strike out at him. "Because they think I am one? Because they read those rags called newspapers and believe that trash?" She was being caustic to keep the fear at bay, but even she could hear the near hysteria in her voice.

"I don't think so," he said calmly, his brown eyes narrowing as he watched her reaction to his next words. "And I don't think you believe that either. Whoever wrote those things has a personal stake or a gripe against you. Someone who read those trashy papers might think it, but they wouldn't go to such lengths to frighten you unless he or she had a grudge against you."

Her face had turned a pale, deathly white. "No," she murmured, almost to herself, but her expression had given her away.

"Who?"

Her voice was so low that it was almost inaudible. "My mother."

Stunned silence filled the room. Catherine turned back to the window, her arms once more folded so that she could hold herself together, like a tightly wound ball of string. Her entire body was singing with a tenseness that made her skin tremble. She had said it out loud. She had admitted for the first time that her mother hated her with such a vengeance that she would try to harm her. She choked back the bile that threatened to rise to her throat. Then she remembered. "Only it couldn't be, because she's in a hospital in Louisiana."

Sam cursed under his breath, his hands reaching out to draw her near only to drop to his sides once more. "Catherine, look at me."

"Go away."

He didn't ask again. With a sense of dread and futility she listened to Sam's receding footsteps as he joined his friends in the back of the house and left her alone.

She closed her eyes, shutting them tight against the thoughts that kept crowding her with visions best left in the past.

Her mother.

Everything she had ever read, ever seen on TV said that mothers were loving and sweet and concerned. Someone who would lead them to a clear-and-set path in life. Someone who cared about them when they were good and even when they were bad.

Then why had God given her to a woman who hated her so much from the moment she was born, she had spilled venom on her like a snake biting its victim? What had Catherine done when she was so young that would make her own mother hate her so?

No matter what she did or how hard she tried, she couldn't find the answer. She could come up with reasons, or excuses, for her mother's behavior in the past, but it still wasn't the same as *knowing*. All Catherine knew was that she was no longer sure if she'd turned out the way she had because that was what she was, in spite of the way she was raised.

Her shoulders slumped. It no longer mattered. Apart from the monthly check Catherine sent her, all communication between them was severed. Neither contacted the other.

Neither wanted to.

And now, this late in her life, she was too exhausted to care anymore. With defeat weighing on her shoulders, she walked to the couch and slumped into the cushions. Somewhere along the line the gods had decided to test her over and over again. Obviously she had failed.

"Catherine, come on." Sam's hand on her shoulder jolted her out of her reverie. "We're going home."

Her head ached. She looked up, her eyes void of expression as he took her hands and stood her on two wobbly feet. "Home? Is it safe?"

"My home is, and that's where you're staying."

"No, I'll stay in a hotel. I'll call my agent," she argued wearily. Suddenly she was coming to life again and losing that blessed numbness that had begun to invade her limbs earlier. She wished for it back. She didn't want to feel, to think, to do. She just wanted to sleep.

Sam's face was lined with hard-edged stubbornness. "No arguments. You're staying with me." He led her down the hall and out the door, his arm possessively around her waist as he walked her toward the car.

They drove in silence, neither attempting to speak. The motor hummed quietly and soon lulled Catherine into a light, dreamless sleep.

The drone of the engine stopped and then her car door opened. She felt Sam's arms envelop her and snuggled into the breadth of his chest, wondering how she could have ever thought it wasn't large. A smile touched her lips, then turned into a whimper as thoughts that lay just beyond her consciousness began to batter once more against her brain.

"Shhh," Sam's low voice soothed as he gently stroked her hair and temples, and she cuddled into his arms again, no longer afraid. Somewhere in the back of her mind she realized that Sam was carrying her from the car into the house, but she was too tired to give it more thought.

Gentle hands removed her clothing and the soft slippery satin of the sheets felt cool on her body. A big, comforting arm held her waist as she curled into a tight ball and drifted into sleep once more.

ONE BLUE EYE OPENED at a time, squinting at the bright morning sunlight pouring in from the undraped window. Catherine focused slowly, unable to see anything but the handsomely sculpted head that leaned over her. It had a funny, lopsided grin that turned up the corners of his mouth, and the corners of his eyes were riddled with the most delightful creases. . . .

"Is this the way you treat a guest?" she murmured, snuggling down into the softness of the sheets and realizing she wore only a pair of panties. Sam must have undressed her and put her to bed. She should have been embarrassed, but she wasn't.

She closed her eyes, hoping to shut out the potency of Sam. It didn't work. She could feel his nearness and smell the tantalizing scent of his after shave. *Careful, Catherine*, something deep inside warned her. He was getting too close to the real Catherine and that was dangerous.

But her senses were still drugged with sleep, for when he leaned forward even more and his lips brushed hers, she unconsciously puckered in readiness. His mouth covered hers, swiftly and possessively. His hands reached to hold her temples and cheeks, his grip tightening as if she were fighting him off.

She didn't move, wanting to feel his mouth, his hands, his tongue. Even more than that, she wanted to feel the delicious weight of his body as it flattened against her breasts. Without thinking, she wound her arms around his neck, pulling him closer, close enough to feel his strength and warmth through the sheet and his shirt.

A tiny moan left her throat to be captured by his mouth. He savored it before giving it back as a small gentle breath.

Her fingernails combed through the tobacco-brown hair that felt so crisp and fresh, and he gave a slight shudder in response to her touch.

His hands left the side of her face to travel to her shoulders, testing, touching, feeling the silkiness of palm against pearlescent skin.

The weight of him was as welcome and delicious as she dreamed it would be, and though he pressed against her breasts, they swelled and peaked for him anyway. She knew that he could feel it, for he rubbed back and forth, reveling in her response.

"Touch me, Catherine," he said in an almost rasping whisper. "Touch me and tell me what you feel."

Without hesitating her hands sloped down his neck to his shoulders, feeling the cording of muscles as he poised over her. He was lean and hard, and the tightness of those muscles felt powerful.

"You're stronger than you look," she said huskily. "You feel good."

"What else?" His lips grazed her neck and cheek, stopping to tantalize her ear with warm breath and teasing words. "What else do you feel?"

"Whipcord strength," she said before her tongue darted out to savor the hollow at his throat. "And you taste like soap."

"I'll lather myself with chocolate if you promise to do that once more," he muttered shakily.

And her tongue darted again to feel the pulse that beat so rapidly. She was being caught up in his magic touch and wondrous words. Her breath was short and her heart pumped as fast as his, giving her a lightheaded feeling that was as heady as a bottle of the best champagne. It was so good. . . .

"And again," he whispered once more, his breathing now coming faster than before. His lips nudged her lobe, teasing it, finally tasting it.

Her hands found his belt and followed the dark leather strap around to the front, knowing before she got there that she would find him aroused and ready. Almost as ready as she was for him. . . .

"Do it, Catherine. Do it, darling." His voice was taut with feeling and she obeyed, knowing she needed his nearness and touch as much as he needed hers.

The belt almost magically undid itself, the snap was next, and then the raucous sound of a zipper filled the air. Sam pulled away momentarily to shed his clothing and then joined her on the bed. Slipping beneath the silken sheets, he gathered her close and rolled her beneath him.

Sam's warmth, the weight of his body on hers, his caressing hands were so very *right* that she had no choice but to fly with him into a never-never land of feelings that overwhelmed. Her sleepy desire for a closeness with another human being had changed into a fiery desire to make love, to be loved, to share love. . . with Sam.

Only Sam.

There were no thoughts in her head, no warnings, no bells that were supposed to peal disaster ahead. Her touch, her emotions, and her light breathing were all done as if she had been programed for this with Sam.

Only Sam.

With mounting tension they claimed the right to pillage the other's body and both met on equal ground. She urged him, taunted him, silently pleaded with him to take her until he was as enraptured as she was and allowed only his feelings to lead him down the path with her. As his hands once more traveled to seek the warmth of her, she arched, knowing that nothing less than being filled with him would do. He accepted her invitation by allowing his lips to nibble at her breast— instead it teased her with more promises of sweet torture. The softness of her legs touching his, her hips moving in silent plea to continue his loving, they all marked her impatience and his undoing. He plunged into her and she met him, thrust for thrust, giving him what he had so wanted to be complete.

When tension mounted to sparks of showering fireworks, Sam's voice echoed in her ear. "So very sweet, so fine..." But she hardly let the words register before climbing her own pinnacle, awed at the wonder of it. Her hands clamped tightly on his shoulders, then suddenly loosened as she felt his tense muscles. They had come together, reached that spot that only lovers do, and shared it as closely as two people could. Slowly, slowly, she came down to land in the safe comfort of his arms.

The need for the feel of his body didn't leave her as Catherine returned from that memorable voyage. She still needed to know he was there, with her, and her arms automatically tightened to keep him at her side.

"I'm not leaving, Catherine. I couldn't," he murmured as he brushed her temple with his lips. A hand trailed down her hip, only this time with reverence, stirring feelings that Catherine had thought were long dead. "You're very special, you know that?"

"How?" Her voice quivered slightly. She silently prayed that he would not come up with all the old clichés. *Please let him tell me the truth,* she asked of the heavens.

"Because you give as good as you get. I gave my best, but so did you." He leaned on one arm to take the weight of himself off, but his brown eyes narrowed as they stared into the confusion of hers. "It made it beautiful, Catherine. Thank you."

No one could have said anything that would have touched her more. For once she didn't set out to disarm or charm. "Thank you."

"Are you hungry?" he asked, his voice still low and seductive.

"What did you have in mind?" she countered. An impish smile lit her eyes and he watched the dark blue change back to the sky blue of an hour ago. "Sam?" Her look was puzzled. What was he thinking that he could get so lost while lying next to her? Was he thinking of another woman? After the beauty of what they had just shared, the thought almost gagged her. She stiffened.

Sam shook his head as if stripping the cobwebs away. "Food," he said as if he had never drifted off, but it was too late.

"Fine. If you'll move, I'll get dressed." Catherine pushed against his shoulders.

Sam was implacable. "Not until I find out what I just said to get you in a snit." His hand tightened on her waist. "What was it? What made you freeze in my arms just now, Catherine? Tell me."

"Nothing," she said, still pushing against one shoulder and getting nowhere. "Move, please."

"Not until you tell me. I said I was hungry, you asked me what for, and I got lost in the blue of your eyes as they changed color. Then you stiffened and tried to push me away. What went wrong?"

Her hands stilled. "'The blue of your eyes as they changed color?' What does that mean? My eyes are always blue." She stared up at him suspiciously, wondering what new turn of events he was handing her now.

He slowly shook his head from side to side, a small smile denting his cheeks. "There must be fifteen shades of blue, and your eyes just went from dark blue to light blue. It was fascinating," he murmured, his eyes still locked with hers.

"That's impossible." She lowered her lashes.

"No, I once read somewhere that it happens in light-eyed people. It has something to do with the blood vessels opening and closing, but I've never seen it happen before. It's remarkable." His hand slipped off her waist to travel up and cup one breast, but his eyes continued to gaze at her. His thumb and forefinger gently tugged at her nipple, sending more messages through her slim body, messages that needed her movements as an answer.

"I thought you were hungry," she said, her voice lowered in the hope that she would have more control over it. She didn't. It still sounded breathless. His touch was doing crazy things to her.

"I am."

"Then, don't you think you ought to move so I can fix us something to eat?"

"No."

"No?" Now her voice was just a whisper of its former self.

"No. I haven't had my fill of this banquet yet." He glanced down at what his hand was doing, then down further to her undulating hips and her slender thighs. Then his eyes pierced hers again. "Have you?"

He had been so honest with her. She had no choice but to be the same with him. "No, I want you again."

For the first time he smiled, really smiled. It was so totally unexpected and so very, very endearing that her heart almost melted from the warmth of it. Her whole body seemed drawn to that wonderful, wide, sensuously wicked smile. "There. At least we're in total agreement about something. This may set a precedent."

And before she could answer, his lips were on hers and her mouth was parting to open like a flower in the brilliant rays of the sun.

A SOFT BREEZE drifted through the open window, gently allowing the loose-weaved curtains to drift back and forth like a sensual dancer. From somewhere in another part of the house, music was playing. It was classical, and Catherine had no idea of its creator. She had never been exposed to classical music before, but strangely enough, she liked the soft, lilting quality of it. It fit with the room, her mood and the moment.

She lay still, listening for other sounds, her mind content to drift along without worry right now. Worry would come later. Now was the time to savor, to touch, to reward herself with...

Her nose twitched. The smell of bacon drifted toward her, making her stomach react with a growl. Then came the scent of freshly brewed coffee. Catherine's imagination played with the rest of the menu. Perhaps Sam had scrambled eggs... or maybe made a batch of muffins... or perhaps fried a few potatoes with onions....

Sam appeared in the doorway, looking more endearing than ever. His hair was slightly damp and his jaw clean shaven. He was wearing a raggedy pair of jean cut-offs and a smile that warmed her with its intimacy. No shirt covered his broad shoulders and lean, slim waist. Dark crisp chest hair disappeared into the low waistband of his shorts. Her imagination picked up the line and drew it from there.

"Good morning," he said huskily, his eyes roaming her body beneath the cover of the sheets, as if he could see right through them and enjoyed what he saw. "Breakfast is almost ready. There's a robe in the closet if you want to put it on."

Catherine grinned back. "Thanks."

"Don't thank me. I'd rather you joined me wrapped in that sheet or better still, nothing. But I have a suspicion that you wouldn't care for that."

She tried to look shocked at his suggestion, but she couldn't pull it off and they both knew it. Giggling, she pulled at the sheet and began wrapping it around her breasts before she slipped from the bed. "I think it's a marvelous idea, Sam," she said primly after she got her giggles under control. "Thanks for the suggestion."

Sam's eyes widened as she stood. The satin molded to her figure like creamy white paint, then flowed down past her feet to spill in rolling folds over the darkness of the carpet. She could have been a statue of a goddess. Her blond hair tumbled in delectable disarray over her shoulders, her eyes wide and bright blue with such a sexy impishness that he wanted to take her in his arms, satin sheet and all, and hold her close. Not make love...just hold her tight enough to imprint his body onto hers so that she would always know that she was irrevocably his.

That last notion jarred him out of his stupor. He had never had a thought like that before, and it scared the hell out of him. But then every thought he'd had since he met the little witch had done that to him.

"Thank goodness we're too old for toga parties," he muttered under his breath. "I'd be fighting all night long." He swallowed twice. Then he turned quickly, forcing a light note over the knot in his throat. "Hurry up, lady. Breakfast will be burned."

Catherine grabbed the train of the sheet and hurried after him, her stomach telling her it was way past time to eat. But her acute disappointment at his apparent lack of reaction to her was what bothered her most.

What was the matter with her? When she'd had him to dinner at her house, she had been pleased that he hadn't seen fit to pour compliments over her like oil on a salad. But now she was angry that he *hadn't* complimented her on her state of dress, or undress, she quietly corrected as she almost tripped over the hem of her toga. Wasn't that what Sam had called it? She wasn't sure, he had mumbled so.

The kitchen was a cook's dream, all bright orange and crisp white, copper pots and cooking implements hanging from the ceiling and walls. The table was laminated white and held orange place mats and clear glass table-ware.

She stood in the doorway, her eyes taking it all in. "Why, it's just like a fresh glass of orange juice!" she exclaimed, her bright blue eyes lighting up in delight.

Sam was standing by the stove, a spatula in his hand. He glanced over his shoulder at her comment, only to stare at the lovely picture she made. No wonder so much had been written about her; she was enough to stir any man and that alone would earn the censure of most women. She was so damn sexy and feminine! He forced himself to grin.

"You like?"

"Oh, Sam, it's beautiful." She looked at him, her eyes locking with his. She tilted her head, her eyes twinkling mischievously. "But can you cook?"

"With all this paraphernalia around, I had to learn, or look like a fool."

She chuckled. "Good! I'm starved!" Without another word she sat down and looked at him patiently but expectantly, as if to ask him where her food was.

He laughed, slipping a perfect omelet on a warmed plate and setting it in front of her. It was garnished with thick slices of bacon and thin slices of fresh orange.

Hands on his hips, he waited for her reaction.

"Ummm, perfect," Catherine murmured, picking up her fork and digging in.

"Just a minute, madam. The chef deserves an award for his efforts, you know." Bending down he brushed his lips across hers. It was supposed to be a quick peck, only the moment he touched her, he knew that he had to have more.

But she pulled away, dipping her head down to receive the first mouthful of eggs.

He grinned at the top of her head. He wanted to touch her, but kept his hands by his sides. She was shy. She was shy! Even after their being together earlier this morning! That didn't fit at all with the image of a conniving, wife-stealing husband the press had created.

Catherine kept her head lowered, knowing her face was beet-red. How could she kiss him back with the fervor she felt when she hadn't even brushed her teeth yet? He had had a chance to clean up, but she hadn't. As soon as she ate breakfast she'd wash up and brush her teeth. Looking up quickly, she saw his smile and couldn't help the smile that lit her own face. Neither moved as they watched the other, grinning like two fat canaries in the same cage.

The ringing of the telephone broke the spell. Catherine jumped and Sam reached for the phone to cut off the sound.

"Hello, Sam Lewis here."

She took another bite of her breakfast, pretending not to be interested in the telephone conversation. Was it a woman? Her eyes traveled the room once more. There was bound to be a dozen women in his life, and probably two dozen trying to make him aware of them. And here she was, sitting in his kitchen looking like a waif and acting like a star-struck child! Where was her polish, her sophisticated veneer, her indestructible wall that she had vowed no man would ever climb over? Obviously it was missing. . . .

"We'll be there in an hour," Sam promised grimly to whomever was on the other end of the line just before he hung up the white wall phone.

The mouthful of food she had just eaten threatened to stick in her throat. A shiver of premonition skittered up her spine. She couldn't look at him, didn't want to hear what she knew he was going to say.

"Catherine?" His voice was soft but implacable.

"Uh-humm?" She still couldn't meet his gaze.

"The police want us to meet them at the house. They need to question you."

"I thought they had done their thing last night?" She picked up a piece of bacon and took a small bite. Two minutes ago it had tasted delicious, now it could have been thick shoelaces.

"They need to talk to you, but I'll be with you." He walked around the table and sat down across from her. "But before we go, I need to know more about your mother." His insides tore a little as he watched the reaction his words had on her.

"No."

"Yes. Last night you said your mother might have done it. Did you mean it?"

"No."

"Then why did you say it?" he prodded gently.

"Because you asked who hated me, and I answered you. But I know my mother didn't do it."

"How can you be so certain?"

Catherine took a deep breath, still staring at her food. Had she really thought she was hungry? "I told you. Because she's in a private hospital in Louisiana. She couldn't be in two places at once."

"Are you sure?"

"Yes." Catherine would *not* go into the details. She kicked herself for being weak enough last night to even mention the hatred her mother held for her.

Sam sighed, running a frustrated hand through his hair. "All right. If you're sure then I won't press." He stood. "While we're there, we'll pick up your clothes and whatever else you need for the next week or so."

Finally she looked up at him. "Does this mean you're my friend or my lover or my attorney?" Her voice was filled with bitterness. He had turned down helping her before. Did he just want her in his bed so he could brag about this relationship later?

Sam leaned over the table, his broad strong hands flat on the surface. Dark brown eyes demanded attention. "It means that I'm all three rolled into one."

"How nice. Less than a week ago you told me I had to find someone else to fill your legal duties," she said tightly, raising one delicate eyebrow. "Did my going to bed with you change your mind?"

He didn't rise to the bait. He could have easily put her in her place with a million come-backs to her smart words, but he also knew enough to see below her surface. "No. I changed my mind."

"I see."

Suddenly his face was even closer than before, making his anger hard to ignore. "The hell you do," he said grimly. "But you will before long, Catherine Sinclair. You will." And with those parting words, he left the kitchen to stalk down the hall toward the bathroom.

Catherine slowly put her knife and fork down and methodically clapped at his dramatic, final exit.

The sound mocked him as it echoed through the house.

6

CATHERINE FELT UNCOMFORTABLE donning the same dressy jump suit she had worn the night before, but she had no choice. As she stepped out of the shower and reached for a towel, she thought about asking Sam if he might have anything appropriate to wear, but she dismissed that notion as quickly as it came. The one thing she wouldn't be able to do was to wear someone else's clothing, especially another woman's, even though she had the feeling there was probably some around here. She didn't need to be reminded that she was just one of the girls, so she was better off not knowing. Where Sam was concerned, her ego was battered enough without hitting herself on purpose.

She quickly applied what little makeup she had in her purse, realizing that she had only brought the essentials with her.

"There's an extra toothbrush in the linen cabinet," Sam shouted through the door, and she yelled back a thanks even as she reached for the handle.

The cabinet's contents made her eyes swim. There had to be at least twenty toothbrushes still in their original packages piled to one side on a shelf. They could have made a colorful bouquet, for every color imaginable was there. That, combined with the rest of the items, stunned her. Electric curlers, hairpins, hairspray, a large economy jar of cold cream, mascara still in its plastic and cardboard wrapper, two tubes of clear lip gloss and...Catherine picked up the last item and stared incredulously at it. In a small clear plastic case sat a pair of carefully trimmed false eyelashes. They were brand new!

"My God," she muttered as she attempted to tamp down the bubbling anger that swelled within her. He had an entire cosmetics market at his fingertips!

Ever since meeting Sam Lewis she'd had the feeling he had struggled with himself concerning his ideas of what she should be versus what she really was. She had been drawn to him, even felt sorry for him at times. She had even thought he might be the only man she'd ever met who was willing to give her the real understanding she needed. The old guilt that used to haunt her had returned when she was with him, his company was so new, so delightful, so fresh. She felt bad because she had memories best left unsaid so it wouldn't sully him. But now. Now she should be able to get a good laugh out of this. Here she was, feeling guilty about her past only to find out she was far more pure than he could ever hope to be!

Visions of his hands caressing her body flashed before her. She stared, unseeing, at the items in front of her. No wonder he was such a good lover. *She* hadn't inspired him to be his best: his undeniable and very well-trained talent with women had insured his ability!

"Uh, Catherine? Let me in and I'll get the toothbrush for you." Sam's voice sounded almost sheepish. Apparently he had just remembered what she would find.

Catherine grabbed a toothbrush and slammed the cabinet door. "Thanks, but I found it," she answered grimly as she walked over to the sink, tearing viciously at the wrapper.

"Let me in, anyway. I want to explain."

"In a pig's eye," she muttered, smearing toothpaste on the offending brush and sticking it in her mouth, barely escaping puncturing her tongue. "Ummmph," she groaned before brushing vigorously.

"Catherine, open the door! I want to talk to you. Now!"

Was that panic that laced his demand? No. She didn't think so.

The door was opened so abruptly that Sam took a step back, expecting a small fist to hurtle toward him. He eyed her warily.

Her hair and lush body were wrapped in primrose yellow towels. Her rosebud mouth was pinched together to resemble a persimmon and there was a toothbrush embedded in it. But her eyes told the real story, and Sam's stomach felt as if it were on an elevator ride...down. They blazed blue sparks at him as if she was willing him to catch on fire.

He still couldn't help chuckling at the picture she made. Then suddenly the fist he had been so wary of earlier struck out to find its way directly to his middle.

A whooshing sound left his lips as the smile quickly disappeared to be replaced with one of surprise.

Catherine stood, hands on hips, toothbrush still in her mouth as she growled in a voice that would have made the Detroit Tigers proud. "Don't you *dare* laugh at me you big, overgrown Casanova! Don't you *dare!*"

If he could have grinned, he would have; the picture before him was so funny. She looked like an overgrown, sunshine yellow, fluff ball who could be picked up and blown away by the wind. Only the light ache in his middle testified to the fact that she was slightly more solid than she appeared.

He knew he deserved the punch, but he wasn't going to let her get away with it! He narrowed his eyes, attempting to look at her as he would a guilty client. "And don't you dare ever hit me again, or I'll take you over my knee and spank you," he said in a deep voice that he hoped held a threatening tone. His eyes narrowed even more. She didn't look the least bit intimidated.

She smiled but the laughter didn't fill her eyes as it usually did. Light blue, they were cold and filled with anger. "Did you want something, Sam? Or were you just scared I'd steal your, your...cosmetics?"

"They aren't mine, and you know it!"

She let out a theatrical sigh. "Oh, I'm so glad. For a minute there I was worried that perhaps you..." She let the thought dwindle off.

That little vixen! She was intimating that *he* used that stuff. And if he admitted out loud that it wasn't his, she'd be proven right as far as his involvements with other women. Tricky little fluff. She paid back as good as she got—with everything.

"Catherine, look. I..." he began, only to be interrupted.

"Did I really hurt you, Sam?" she asked softly. "I'm sorry. I guess I just let your...your ministore get me upset. Will you forgive me?" Her eyes were wide, the toothbrush now in her hand instead of almost protruding from her cheek. She looked so clean and sweet and fluffy.

He smiled slowly, giving it his charming all. "Sure. And about the drugstore in there—" his eyes shot to the now-closed cabinet "—it's not my stuff, it's April's. She used to live here and just never picked it up." Then he smiled brightly, hoping he'd alleviated her suspicions.

Catherine's blue eyes widened even more. "April? As in April and Jace?"

Sam nodded, unable to take his eyes from hers. They were so blue and so vulnerable. "Before she and Jace married, they had a difference of opinion and April moved in for a while."

Catherine smiled sweetly again. "Oh, really? How nice for you," she said softly.

"It wasn't that way. April and I have been friends for a long time. Where else would she go but to a friend when she needed one?"

Catherine walked back to the sink and rinsed out her mouth. Wiping daintily with a third towel, she looked over her shoulder at him. "Does Jace know?"

"Of course."

"And does April have other fetishes? I mean besides carrying around hair curlers when her hair is so short, and a dozen or so toothbrushes?" Catherine's voice was still sweet and innocent sounding, but Sam could smell a trap a mile away.

"No. I do," he said calmly, crossing his arms and leaning against the doorjamb.

She unwrapped her hair from the towel and shook her head, allowing the damp locks to tumble in disarray on her now sweet-smelling shoulders.

Sam stood a little straighter, the ache in his stomach had disappeared as an ache in his loins had begun. She looked so soft, so sweet, so delectable . . . she looked like a little blond, cuddly, curvy ball of fluff. He dropped that thought, reminding himself of the strength of her punch.

She took the comb from her purse and began combing the tangles from her hair, arching her neck and curving her spine in delicious ways. Her eyes met his in the mirror and she slowly, sensuously smiled, the promise of another night shining brightly in her sky-blue eyes. All thoughts of the previous conversation left his mind as he became drawn into her gaze.

"Sam? Are we...friends?" she asked softly.

"Of course." He swallowed.

Her eyes dropped. "Thank you," she said.

It wasn't until they were in the car and headed toward Catherine's rental house that he wondered about her quick turn of behavior. Normally he would never have allowed a woman access to that cabinet, but he hadn't been thinking clearly. It took too many explanations and much soothing for most women to cope with his life-style. Other women would have questioned the toothbrushes more closely, putting him on the defensive or making themselves such nuisances that he would have taken them home and not asked them out again. He smiled. But then Catherine was a woman of the world and didn't need to question closer. She knew the game. She probably hadn't given the toothbrushes another thought....

THAT DAMN MAN! Catherine fumed all the way to the house. She was exhausted, angry and frustrated, and all because of him.

Who did he think he was? Her shining star? Fat chance! Her lover? Not on a bet! She wouldn't stand in line for anyone. Her friend? Hardly! A friend didn't put

you in line for loving, but gave it freely when you needed it.

That thought led to another that almost jolted her out
of her seat. Was she going crazy? She had never had
friends! Friends were people who asked you for things,
who knew too much about you and turned on you when
it came down to the wire. She put friends in the same
category as she put family—both should be shared by
someone else. But not her. Never her.

A bitter taste entered her mouth. She must have been
under a spell these past few days or she never would
have succumbed to Sam's charms. Exhausted she was,
but crazy she wasn't. Her relationship with Sam would
wind up quickly; as soon as they found the thief who
was breaking into her house and destroying her peace of
mind. Until then she would use him. After that, she
didn't care if he lived or died as long as he wasn't taking
up space in her backyard. The old toughness was returning. She'd make it and she'd make it on her own.
She didn't need anyone's help, especially a woman-
chasing attorney who probably needed another notch
on his bedpost just to keep up his morale! And especially one who placed the blame on an innocent woman!
Poor April. If Sam was her best friend, she was in deeper trouble than she knew!

They began ascending the canyon road and her
thoughts turned away from Sam to the house she had
rented. Last night had been the most terrifying night of
her life.

When her necklace had been stolen there was the pos-
sibility that she had left the door unlocked. But last
night she knew the house had been locked and bolted.
There was no accidental latch left undone, no window

left open for ventilation. She had triple checked everything before going out.

Someone had the key.

But who? She had told Sam about her mother, but even in her deepest fear she hadn't really believed it was her. Besides, she paid the hospital bills and her accountant kept track of everything for her, so he would have known if her mother had left the sanitarium and when.

Her mother.

She hadn't even been that terrified when she'd watched her mother and stepfather stumble and curse their anger at the injustices of life and then finally pass out from cheap liquor bought by the case, thanks to their daughter's paycheck as a sweeper and cleaner at the local hairdresser's. That hadn't been terror in those days, it had been disgust and fear of the future.

This was different. Who would write those horrid things about her? True, they were the same things her mother used to throw into the air in a fit of temper, but whoever wrote these things had an inbred hate for her. She might not be anyone's idea of the perfect woman, but she certainly had not deserved those awful insults.

She tensed, realizing just how close they were coming to the driveway that read Castaways on the burnt wood sign. Something, some faraway thought in the back of her mind tickled her memory, but she couldn't bring it forward. That was almost as frightening as the robbery.

As they pulled into the driveway, Sam's hand came across the seat and covered hers, giving a light squeeze. She turned her head sharply, surprised at his thoughtfulness after the thoughts she'd been having earlier.

"It'll be all right, Catherine. The police are there," he said reassuringly.

"I know," she answered, wishing her voice wouldn't sound so shaky. One year ago she would have sounded cool no matter what had happened, but her extreme exhaustion and mental state weren't conducive to cool voice and even cooler thoughts. She felt scattered, indecisive, unable to cope with everything at once.

The police photos had already been taken and the mirrors erased, thank goodness. And only the uniformed officers were there. They sat in the living room smoking cigarettes and lounging in the chairs as they awaited their superior officer.

As Catherine and Sam walked in, Sam gave her hand another squeeze, telling her once more that she wasn't alone. She squeezed back, unwilling to analyze why she felt so comforted by his presence.

"Miss Sinclair, if you like, you have time to freshen up before Sergeant Donovan returns. He said he'd be back within the hour," the younger man said, his eyes staring admiringly at the small, but very feminine, blonde in front of him.

She smiled. This man, like most, she could handle. "Thank you. Why doesn't someone put on a pot of coffee? I'm sure you could use a little refreshment."

His grin widened even more as he ambled past her toward the kitchen. As he reached the door he turned to take one more look at her, and, with an audacity that reminded her of earlier days, she winked.

He blushed, then winked back before practically swaggering through the doorway.

Sam's hand dropped hers as if it were on fire. She ignored him even though the tension flowed from his body to enfold her like a sticky cocoon. Dammit! He had no right to tie her up as if she were a package to be placed under his Christmas tree. He had no right! She *had* to show him that she wasn't a man's possession. She held no strings on him and certainly didn't want strings attached to her.

"Excuse me," she murmured as she turned toward the staircase and began the ascent to her room.

Sam's voice interrupted her path. "Don't forget to pack a suitcase of whatever you'll need at my house... darling," he said with an intimate note in his voice.

She bristled. Stopping on the fifth step and looking down her nose autocratically, because she was taller than he was, she frowned. "I'll think about your generous offer of a room, Mr. Lewis. I haven't made up my mind, yet."

"Oh, yes you have, darling. Don't play games in front of the police. They already know you've been with me since the robbery and will be with me until this is solved." This time his voice was laced with a promise... probably to beat her if she didn't play his way!

"We'll see," she murmured as she continued on upstairs. His nerve was worse than her own. How dare he embarrass her that way. How dare he push her into situations she neither made nor wanted. The pig! The male chauvinist pig! She slammed her bedroom door, sending him her message with sound. He was probably laughing at her with those policemen right now. He was probably telling them...

Common sense came to the fore. No, he wasn't. Sam might be a lot of things, but he certainly wasn't vindictive. She had served him and his suggestion on a platter, and he had just served it back.

The anger drained as quickly as it had come. Next came a small giggle as she remembered his jealousy with the policeman. Sam had been downright angry! But anger wasn't the reason for his announcing their living arrangement. Trying to put him in his place had made him stand up to her. He might be a bit possessive, but he wasn't ordinarily rude. If she hadn't pushed, he wouldn't have shoved back. And she knew it.

She entered the bathroom and began washing her hands and face, letting the cool water soothe her skin.

Ever since she had met the man, Sam had been an enigma. He was so honest and open in his emotions, so earnest in his approach. She had been the one playing games. Suddenly the smile left her face. She had always been the one playing games: dreaming, wishing, manipulating others. And she had been the one who had gotten hurt. A bad taste of the past entered her mouth and she quickly swallowed.

She grabbed a towel from the rack and patted her face dry. She didn't want to think of all the things she had done wrong. She didn't want to feel those guilt feelings pile up until she could hardly breathe or look another person in the face. When that happened, she could hardly cope....

The click of the door told her that Sam was standing there, watching her. She ignored him although she could hardly disregard the racing of her pulse and her quickened breathing.

Placing the towel back on the rack, she began fumbling in her makeup drawer. The only sound was the clink of bottles being moved about. Still he said nothing.

She didn't glance at him, but her peripheral vision told her that he was lounged against the doorjamb, arms crossed. He looked totally relaxed but she knew it wasn't so, for tension still emanated from him.

Finally she couldn't take it any longer. "Did you want something?" she asked with distinct disinterest as she lightly stroked a pencil on her brow.

"Yes."

"What?"

"You."

A shiver went down her spine with the meaning of that one word. She placed the pencil carefully on the counter and turned to look at him for the first time. She raised one brow, her mouth curving into the semblance of a mocking smile. "Really? That doesn't make you special, Sam," she said softly but with threaded steel underneath.

"Oh, but it does," he answered, equally softly. His eyes narrowed as he gave her the same hint of a smile she had given him. Her spine stiffened. She was on dangerous ground, only she wasn't sure why.

"How so?"

"Because you've never been with a man like me before, and you know it."

This time her brows raised in honest surprise. She had underestimated his ego. And she had underestimated her own reaction to him. But she bluffed, anyway. "And what makes you so special? Your money? Your position? Your expertise as a lover?" Her voice was derisive.

"Because I take you as you are: a bitchy, sometimes nice, sometimes scared, sometimes lonely woman. I've seen parts of your personality that no one else has seen. I've seen you at your best. . .and at your worst."

"And what makes you the expert?" She turned back

to the mirror to place blush on her now white cheeks. Her hand shook slightly as she held the large, fluffy, sable brush.

"Far more women in my life than men in yours. You're a quick learner, Catherine. If there had been more men in your life for you to learn from, you'd know what I know about the opposite sex." His tone had turned conversational, his smile more relaxed.

"I've learned enough," she snapped, dropping the brush on the counter. "At least enough to know that you're a pompous ass to think you can read *my* thoughts and *my* emotions!" Her temper was ripe now. Was he so stupid that he couldn't understand her anger?

Not a muscle in Sam's face tightened. In fact, if anything, he was smiling wider. "Don't underestimate me, Catherine. I'm easygoing and relaxed most of the time. I enjoy the banter that can only come between two people who can connect on more than one level, such as you and I can. But I have a tenacity that matches yours, otherwise neither of us would be where we are right now. Start thinking of me as a fan and I'll know you're less bright than I've given you credit for."

He *was* laughing at her! Heat filled her body, charging through her head until she could barely see. No one laughed at her! No one! Without being conscious of what she was doing, she slapped his face, the sharp sound echoing around the tiled room.

Sam didn't move a muscle; he just watched her through narrowed lids as she began trembling.

"I'm sorry," she whispered, fear snaking through her body. Tears pierced the corners of her eyes.

"I'm not," he said in a low voice. "You wouldn't have gotten so upset if I hadn't pushed you." His hands reached out and grasped her shoulders as he continued to stare into her eyes. "But I will never stand still for you to slap me again. Remember that." His fingers tightened their hold. "I said that I'd spank you if you ever did that again. Well, I've got a better idea."

With lightning quick movement his head lowered and he claimed her lips, ruthlessly searching her mouth for the truth of her reactions. She answered just as fervently as he questioned, her arms wrapping around his neck to draw him even closer to her, hugging him like a talisman to ward off evil spirits. Tears coursed down her cheeks as she gave him back kiss for kiss, touch for touch. Her hands frantically searched his hair, his neck, his shoulders for purchase.

Her movements were slowed by his own. He took her hands in his and held one to his chest to feel his beating heart, while the other he held close to his jaw. He needed her touch as much as she needed his presence. Were they both casting spells to ward off ghosts or were they really becoming necessary to each other? Catherine didn't know. But the beat of his heart against the palm of her hand was like a lullaby to her nerves. Sam was here, Sam was here.

"Oh, Catherine, you're going to come to me without those walls. Soon. I can feel it," he muttered brokenly, finally resting his forehead against hers as his lips teased the tip of her nose. His hips delved gently into hers, swaying from side to side with a mesmerizing rhythm. "Feel that. That's what you do to me day and night. All you have to do is walk across the room and I'm dying inside to touch you like this, hold you against me."

His confession echoed the hunger in her stomach and

she swayed toward him, feeling his need build with just a few motions.

"Do you even begin to understand just how much we need each other?" he questioned, his breath now stirring the tendrils of her hair.

She leaned back to gaze up at him. His eyes were half closed and there was such a look of vulnerability about him. But she steeled herself to say what she had to say. "No, Sam. There's a big difference between need and want. I want you, I can't hide that fact. But I don't need you. I don't need anyone." She stood taller, forcing her body to pull away from his. Her blue eyes stared up at him, daring him to challenge her. "I will never, ever need anyone."

Her voice held so much conviction that Sam was momentarily shaken. Then slowly he relaxed, forcing his breath to come more evenly. "You'll need me, Catherine Sinclair. Before this is all over, you'll need me." His voice held the promise of that threat, and she cringed at the thought of being dependent on anyone again. The words seemed to hover about her before Sam's hands dropped to his side and he turned and walked away, leaving her terribly alone in the now empty room.

She waited fifteen minutes before she finally moved toward the staircase to go through the ordeal of the interview with the police. Trying to focus all her concentration on the interrogation ahead was harder than anything she had done. Sam's face, his heavy-lidded eyes filled with tenderness and need kept bursting into her brain. Feelings that were so confused she couldn't separate them into compartments filled her with more conflicting emotions. Everything was so complicated!

Sam met her at the bottom of the stairs, his eyes

searching hers before he took her hand and led her into the living room. They sat on the couch and faced the officer in charge, Catherine quietly answering the questions as best she could.

It didn't take more than half an hour and it was over. Sam, confirming with the officer that all locks would be changed and new locks placed on the windows, hastily packed her suitcase himself and ushered her out to the car.

She leaned against the headrest and closed her eyes, wishing herself on a desert island. The questions had brought back all the fear of last night when she'd walked in the house and had seen the scrawlings on the mirror. It trembled through her like wind through an aspen, leaving her shivering and shaking. It also confirmed another fear: the one that said she wasn't strong enough to hold her own. Would she ever be again?

"They know the entry wasn't forced. There wasn't a mark anywhere on the doors or windows. Because it's a rental house, they'll have to find out how many people had the key to it. Since it's been rented so often and the locks haven't been changed in over three years, it will take time." Sam's voice cut into her thoughts and brought her back to the present.

"I know," she answered tiredly, opening her eyes but not moving her head.

"You're safe now, Catherine. It's all over as far as you're concerned."

She nodded, too exhausted to argue with him. If it was over then why didn't she feel better? Why this dark cloud of dread that seemed to permeate her very skin? Was it because she was tired and rundown? Was it because she felt so very, very fragile? She gave a sigh. She didn't know and couldn't find answers that would put to rest those haunting questions.

As Sam pulled the car into his driveway, he glanced at her. Her face was white, her eyes shadowed with a fear that only she knew the reason for. Visions of her lost to him crept into his thoughts, and he felt upset at his inability to help her overcome her reaction to this mess.

He took the keys from the ignition, but neither of them made a move to leave the close confines of the car. He turned in his seat, his head just inches from hers.

"Catherine?"

She stared at him, her head still relaxed against the headrest. "Hmm?"

He smiled. "Nothing. Just...Catherine."

"Sam," she breathed quietly.

"Hmm?"

"Nothing. Just...Sam."

When his lips first touched hers they were so gentle they could have been a mere breeze. One, two, three times he kissed her to reassure her of his presence, and three times she allowed him to give her sustenance.

Her hand came up and cradled the side of his jaw, her long nails touching the outline, the pads of her fingers feeling the tight strength of his flesh. It was the most intimate caress he had ever felt.

He looked into her sky-blue eyes and saw himself. And his feelings for Catherine suddenly crystalized. He loved her. It was wonderful and awe-inspiring. It was the most frightening and depressing thing he had ever experienced. With that thought came another. He would make her love him. He would force her to see that they needed each other to complete their lives.

God couldn't have made him capable of loving so deeply and then take away the one he loved. He couldn't! All Sam had to do was be patient with Catherine while he made her realize that he was the only man she would ever need or want.

Why did he suddenly feel like a mountain climber without a safety rope?

7

CURLED UP IN SAM'S BED, sleep came easily to Catherine, just like it used to when she was a young girl. Whenever she had been depressed or lonely she would fall into a deep sleep, only wandering in and out of the real world long enough to eat and shower before going back into the dream world of oblivion. Now was no exception..

She could feel Sam's presence near her, and that alone gave her a sense of peace she hadn't known for years. It reminded her of their first night together, when he had held her in his arms all night so she could sleep.

She dreamed again.

Her moans tried to escape her throat but nothing happened. Her throat had closed up on her and she couldn't utter a sound. She ran, ducking and weaving through the tenement's narrow, garbage-filled alleys. Her lungs hurt, her breathing was sharp as broken glass. Someone was following, gaining on her. They ran with long strides that pounded into the pavement and echoed in her head. She ducked, then took off again, weaving in and out of the alleys that made her home.

Suddenly arms encased her, stopping her frantic movements and she panicked. "No!"

"Shhh. It's all right." Sam's voice entered and passed through the fog of the nightmare to pull her slowly but steadily to the safety of his arms, his bedroom. "You're with me, Catherine. You're safe," he crooned as he rocked her against his chest to shoo away whatever had frightened her so. His hands gently rubbed her back, soothing her almost as much as his low voice.

Her still-trembling hand came up to cup his jaw. Her eyes strained through the darkness to see his face. It took a moment to focus, then she saw him. His wonderful, rugged, lean face, so full of love and honesty.

He smiled and suddenly the room wasn't dark anymore. His lips parted to show even white teeth. "Is the trembling because of me, or is it the dream?" he asked quietly, but there was a hint of teasing in his voice.

"The dream," she whispered.

"Damn. I was hoping you were finally succumbing to my charms." His voice still held a teasing note, but she could feel the truth of his words.

"Why?" she asked slowly. Her dreams were behind her now, disappearing quickly as they usually did when she awoke. Now there was Sam in front of her, holding her, and he was real. He was needed.

"Because I think you're pretty special, lady, and I'd like you to think the same about me."

She tilted her head, her eyes finally adjusting to the dim light the opened bedroom door allowed entrance. "I don't know what to make of you, Sam Lewis. You've never reacted the way I expect most men to act. Do you do the unexpected on purpose?"

"Always," was his prompt reply. "It keeps the women on their toes."

"And allows you to waltz them into this bedroom long enough for you to make love to them and let them use your stash of toothbrushes," she finished for him, a bitter note entering her voice.

"Before, yes."

"Before what?"

His eyes searched hers. His pulse was beating strongly against her palm as it rested on his neck. "Before you," he said simply and honestly.

His directness unnerved her. "Sam, hold me," she whispered, feeling a deep chill settle into her bones. She didn't want to leave him, and yet the need she felt for him, the same need that had kept her here, frightened her. It frightened her more than the burglar in her home or the thought of her too demanding career. . . .

SUNDAY PASSED with such peace and contentment—both of them putting aside any arguments that could disrupt the tranquility—that it took everything Sam had to pull himself into the office on Monday. It was especially hard for him since the morning had bloomed as if God gave only one good day a year, and this was it. There was no smog, no heavy humid wind, no burning high temperature. It was just right.

Nevertheless, Sam left for work at his usual time, warning Catherine against answering the phone, preferring the answering service to do so unless he gave her a signal, two short rings, which meant he'd hang up then call again. Even though she promised to follow his instructions, he was worried. After the toothbrush episode, he didn't need for her to find anything else wrong with him. And the women who might call would probably be only too happy to set Catherine straight as far as his love life was concerned. Catherine was already balking at being in his home, he didn't need anything negative to happen now.

He had come up with one or two more reasons to delay his departure, but when he saw the twinkle in Catherine's eyes, he knew she'd seen through him and left without another word.

But after an hour at the office he still hadn't accomplished anything. He realized that he should be working, but there wasn't a bone in his body that wanted to make a move toward that direction. His thoughts were completely absorbed with Catherine. Staring at the wall in front of his desk, he twisted paper clip after paper clip into a work of art, discarding each, then beginning again. The files on the corner of his desk remained undisturbed.

"I see you're really whipping through your cases this morning, counselor." Brenda stood in the doorway, her bright teasing smile pulling one from him. "Everything all right?"

"Fine," he said, still twisting the wire in his hand. "If you can call one disaster after another 'fine.'"

"Anything I can do to help? Would you like to dictate some answers to a few of the letters you received in the mail?" she prompted. Ignoring disasters was her favorite thing.

"No way," he said, finally throwing another paper clip in the trash. His brow furrowed. "Brenda, how hard would it be to get this week off? Is my schedule crowded or can things be postponed?" He stood as if suddenly making a decision. "Is April in? Do I have to be in court?"

Brenda tilted her head to one side as she thought, then, as if to confirm, she reached toward his desk and flipped his personal calendar quickly as her mind flew to her own work load. "April's not in, she's in court with a palimony case. Your schedule is light compared to next week. With the exception of a lunch on Wednesday with Leo Coulter, which I suppose you could cancel, and a meeting on Thursday, everything can be moved. You have no court cases this week." She placed her hip against the desk and watched him pace, a small frown on her face.

"Good. I need, no, deserve a week off. Do that for me, please?" He grinned at the thought of having the week with Catherine. In fact, he felt better already, as if a weight had just been lifted from his shoulders.

"Sure, but..." She hesitated a moment, her hazel eyes showing indecision. "Will you tell April?"

"Yes," he said, still grinning. Knowing that April would never hurt a fly, it was a mystery to him why Brenda never even wanted to look as if she were crossing her. "Did April give you a hard time last week?"

Brenda shrugged. "No, but she's been highs and lows for several days. First she walks around with a smile on her face, then she begins crying over the slightest thing. If I didn't know any better, I'd say she was pregnant."

Sam's face showed his surprise. "Pregnant?"

"Yes, you know. A little Jace Sullivan dangling on Uncle Sam's knees." Brenda grinned.

"I know, but I doubt if that's the trouble. April never said a thing about it."

"Oh, and of course she would discuss it with you, Sam. She would have raced to your home, intruded upon your houseguest and told you about it immediately." She hesitated just a fraction of a second before she inquired, "You *do* have a guest in your house?"

"Yes." He waited.

"Don't you think you might enjoy getting out and having some time for yourself?"

"Exactly. That's why I want this week off. I want to show Catherine some of California."

Brenda's brows rose. "In less than three days' time?"

"What are you talking about?"

"The locksmith called this morning and said that he'd be finished with Catherine Sinclair's house by Wednesday night, so she'd be able to go home then."

Sam turned to the window to gaze down at the street scene below. Cars passed back and forth on the streets, people hurried along, not even paying attention to the wonderful weather. He wanted to be like Dorothy and click his heels and be home with Catherine. "That's fine, Brenda. I'll tell her." Later. Much later.

"Sam, is everything all right?" She couldn't ignore the obvious. This wasn't the usual Sam. "Are you sick?"

"No. Yes. Hell, I don't know." He turned and looked at her with eyes filled with sadness and indecision. "I'm in love and I'm damned if I know what to do about it." He shook his head as he stared at his highly polished shoes. "It's all wrong. She's the wrong woman for me and I'm definitely the wrong man for her. And to top it all off, this is the wrong time!"

Comprehension filled Brenda's eyes. "So that's it!" She grinned knowingly from ear to ear. "I knew the day would come when you'd fall in love, I just didn't realize it would be this hard on you. But you deserve it, Sam Lewis. You deserve every little painful bit of it!"

"Me?" His surprised tone made Brenda smile even more. "What did I ever do to deserve going through this hell?"

"You flitted through life as if you were the only bee and every woman was a flower just waiting to cross-pollinate. Now the tables have turned."

His face resembled a thundercloud. "Maybe, but if this is what love is supposed to be like, then it's sadly overrated," he growled.

"Yup, it's love all right," Brenda confirmed unnecessarily to the room.

"And I don't deserve it," Sam continued, ignoring her statement. "I never hurt anyone. In fact, I think I gave as much pleasure as they did."

Brenda groaned. "Not only is it love, it's also a man speaking. No one else could be so conceited."

He glared at her. "Have you ever heard any complaints?"

"Yes, plenty. All from women who wanted the secret to your heart. They were more anxious about trying to please you than you pleasing them. You'd be amazed at the free lunches I get from women hoping to pump more information about you out of me."

"That's *because* I pleased them, not in spite of it," Sam corrected her.

She shrugged. "Okay. But I still say it's time. By the way, who's the 'lucky' woman?"

He hesitated only a moment before giving her a challenging look. "Catherine Sinclair."

Brenda's expression was one of deep shock. Her mouth opened, her jaw moved, but no sound came forth. Finally she spoke. "My God, there's no chance in the world it will work." Her voice was a hoarse whisper, reflecting her awe of the complications she saw ahead.

Sam grunted, then turned and began pacing the room. It wasn't exactly the response he had expected, but he certainly wouldn't probe it. Better that he keep his own council right now than listen to Brenda give him instructions on love and its pitfalls. He saw enough of them without her help.

"You don't even make as much money in a year as she does in a month. She'll have you changing careers, changing life-styles. Changing, period."

He ignored that remark.

"Just get me out of my appointments for the week, Brenda, and when April calls, tell her she can reach me at home."

Brenda nodded then carefully closed the door behind her. There were messes and then there were messes, but this was the biggest one she had seen.

Sam was usually a great boss. The work load was sporadic, either feast or famine, but Sam often helped her beyond the normal boss-secretary relationship. She admired him for caring, she liked him for sharing, and she enjoyed his escapades with women. He deserved more than Catherine Sinclair. Much more. Sam didn't know it, but he was really the type to have a comfortable home life with lots of kids and a doting wife. He wasn't the glamorous, Hollywood, jet-set type that Catherine was. He could never be.

But then she wasn't one to give advice, either. She had already loused up her own life by marrying a man who didn't really believe in marriage. Five years and three children later, he finally found the woman of his dreams...someone else's very wealthy and better-looking wife.

SAM DIALED his home number quickly, hung up, then dialed again. At her sexy-voiced hello, his stomach tensed. His heartbeat sped up to double time. He had to play it cool. "Catherine? How are things going?" He cursed himself for sounding so much like a juvenile. What a stupid opening!

"Just fine. Do you mind if I use up your flour? You don't have much left and I wanted to try my hand at some baking. . . ." Her voice drifted off when she didn't hear his affirmation.

He cleared his throat, forgetting for a moment that he had to answer, getting lost in the images that her voice created. "That sounds great. By the way, I'm taking the rest of the day off so I'll be home in a couple of hours."

Her voice sounded relieved. "Wonderful. We'll talk about it when you get home."

"Fine," he clipped, almost afraid to say more. "See you then."

Visions of Catherine in his kitchen filled him with joy. She had said that she would see him at home! Their home, he thought with great satisfaction.

THREE HOURS LATER Sam slipped the key to his door in the lock. He was almost afraid to open it in case Catherine had decided to leave. Despite his bravado, his thoughts were constantly projected toward losing her before he proved to her that his love was enough for both of them. He'd be good for her, he knew it. He'd make himself good for her.

The house was permeated with the scent of spices and mouth-watering dishes. She must have been cooking all morning. He leaned against the front door savoring the smell.

"Sam? Is that you?" Catherine came to the kitchen door, her eyes bright. A dash of flour streaked one cheek, a delightful smile tilted her mouth becomingly.

"Yes," he said, more affected by her presence than he

could ever hope to contain. He swallowed hard to get rid of the lump in his throat.

Catherine stepped into the hallway, a wooden spoon in one hand. She was wearing a pair of white shorts and a pale green top, and looked sophisticated and charming. And heart-stoppingly beautiful. "Are you all right?"

He couldn't speak; he just nodded his head. How could he tell her how wonderful it was to come home from work and find her here? How very *right* her being here was? He couldn't find the words. He silently held out his arms.

Without a second's hesitation, she was in them, her arms wrapped around his waist, her head resting against his chest.

They were both home.

DINNER WAS QUIET but delicious. Catherine had made a pot roast with potatoes and carrots and a large tossed salad. For dessert she had baked a large coffee cake with raisins and nuts and cinnamon. They drank iced tea laced with fresh mint.

Sam leaned back, replete, a small smile of contentment etching his mouth in a fascinating way. "Tell me about you," he coaxed, watching her relax.

"Nothing much to tell." Her hand twisted around the glass but her eyes never looked up at him.

"Tell."

"I love to cook, read romances and mysteries, sing, and vacuum."

His brows rose. "Vacuum? I didn't know it was considered a hobby."

"It's the most relaxing one. You push and pull a thing

across the floor and it does the work while your mind blanks out."

"Do you do this very often?"

"When I'm on vacation, I could do it at least five times a day and not be satisfied. Now your turn. What are you like?"

"I love to read romances and mysteries, sing off tune and sit in a hot-tub."

She chuckled. "Do you read romances to give you new ideas?"

"No, just to help me figure out the female mind," he countered. "Do you read mysteries to give you new ideas?"

"Yes. Since most heros in mysteries are men, I'm trying to figure out the logic behind the male mind," she answered. Her brow furrowed. "But you don't have a hot-tub."

"I know. If I had one I'd probably never get to work, so I visit friends and borrow theirs." He remembered what Brenda said today about his lack of money and he quickly reassured her. "I could afford one, I just know that I wouldn't be as productive with it around."

"I see," Catherine murmured slowly. "Does that mean that you supply those who allow you the use of their hot-tub the prize of a spanking new toothbrush in the color of their choice?"

"Never mind," he muttered, taking a swig of his iced tea. He glanced down at his glass and then back at Catherine. "Would you mind if I had a glass of wine?" His look was innocent enough, but she could tell he was waiting for her reaction.

"Of course not," she said calmly. "I'm not a drinker

so I don't always remember that others might like it." She gave him her best smile.

But he persisted. "Do you not like the taste or is it against your religion?"

"Neither." Her smile was drooping and she knew it, but she valiantly kept up the attempt, hoping he would drop the subject.

"Then why?"

Her first thought was to tell him it was none of his business, but she knew that wouldn't work. Besides, he had always been honest with her and for some reason—which she didn't want to examine under a microscope—she wanted to be equally honest with him. His was a natural curiosity. What harm could it do to tell? "My parents were alcoholics. I guess I'm afraid that I'll take after them. The easiest way to avoid it is not to drink at all."

"Did you ever drink?"

She nodded slowly, her mind flitting back over the years while she was struggling with her public life and her private love. "Yes. And made a big fool of myself every time by doing things I never would have normally done. Then one day I woke up and said 'no more.'"

"And turned over a new leaf."

She grinned. "A trite saying, but yes."

"Was this long ago?"

"Are you a psychiatrist?"

Now it was his turn to grin sheepishly. "No, just a very interested male trying to learn what makes a very interesting female tick."

"Then read another romance," she said. "As women go, we're all pretty much the same."

"Touché," he murmured, lifting his glass of tea. Suddenly he had lost his taste for wine. But he hadn't lost his taste for Catherine. If anything, his hunger had grown all day until it filled him like a muted ache in the pit of his stomach, flowing through his body like warm, sweet, maple syrup.

AFTER DINNER, Sam took her through the neighborhood, walking slowly, talking slower, both enjoying the sunset as they meandered along the sidewalk. He took her arm when they crossed streets, guided her when they turned corners, but that was the extent of his contact with her. He wasn't sure if he was punishing himself or her, but it was exquisite torture. They spoke occasionally, but the silences were just as sweet.

Once they stopped to watch a group of neighborhood children making a parade. Wagons, bikes and trikes were adorned with streamers and their respective owners were decked out in their parents' old, cast-off clothing. A young boy in his father's old suit with a knotted tie around his neck and dangling over his small bare chest, tipped his hat and gave a wide grin.

Sam chuckled, but when he looked at the expression on Catherine's face, his arm instinctively circled her waist. Whatever deep emotion she was feeling both touched and hurt her. He could see it in her eyes, feel it in the stiffness of her body.

Back at the house they watched TV together, neither saying much. Tension built in the air like a child's set of blocks, one at a time. All he wanted to do was reach over and steal a kiss from her lips, but he didn't have the nerve to do so unless she gave him some sign, any sign, that she was willing. Occasionally he would stare at the wall above the TV and practically will her to say something to him that he could take as encouragement, but nothing happened, adding to his frustration.

By ten o'clock Catherine's head was nodding.

"Catherine? Go to bed," he said softly in her ear, hoping for just one moment she would instead curl up in his lap.

"Good idea," she mumbled, standing before he could help her. "Good night."

He listened to her walking down the hall and into the bedroom, his heart sinking as he heard the door close. She hadn't gone into his room. She had entered the guest bedroom. Seconds later he heard the click of the small lock on the door, and his heart sank even more. She was silently telling him to stay away from her.

Why? Was he some kind of monster? Did he look like he was going to attack her? Didn't she trust him? He had to almost chuckle at the last thought. How could she trust him when he didn't trust himself around her? She must have felt the tension in the air, the urgency in his body. She had to have known and silently made her decision.

He gave a heavy sigh and began walking around the house, making sure the lights were out and the door and windows locked. He had subtly tried to push her, and she was pushing back the same way.

Give her time, his conscience said, but his body was impatient. In all fairness, he didn't just want to make love to her, he wanted to hold her close, to protect her, to let her feel that he had enough love for two.

He stripped naked and climbed into bed. Folding his arms behind his head, he stared at the ceiling. He told his body to unwind but it wasn't receiving the message. His muscles were tightly coiled and ready to react to the slightest sound.

Well, he'd give her time, if that's what she needed. But it wouldn't be his fault if he dwindled away to only a shadow of his former self by the time she was through with the havoc she played on his nerves!

CATHERINE LAY IN BED and listened to the sounds Sam made as he closed the house for the night. She had been sleepy as she had sat with him on the couch, but it had been a sleepiness caused by complete contentment and security. Once she had chosen to sleep in this room instead of his, though, her sleepiness had vanished. Now she was wide awake and hungering for his touch.

She had entered the guest room because she was afraid of Sam. Oh, not in the usual sense, for he was as gentle and kind as anyone she had ever met before. But she knew she was getting too attached to him and that frightened her. Everything seemed to frighten her these days. But especially Sam. She was relying on him when she should be relying on no one but herself. The present situation was too comfortable and she knew it had to come to an end.

Why, her other self asked, and she attempted to come up with an answer that wasn't built on panic.

Because there is too much of a difference between us to bridge the gap.

Baloney, was her other self's answer.

Because he's the type that wants a "forever."

Is that why he's had so many women floating through his life? Is that why he has toothbrushes in his linen closet, her other self questioned.

No, but he was after her. He was like a missile honing in on her. He'd get through her radar and smash her to smithereens before she could retaliate.

Was that the real reason she was afraid of him? Or was it something so elementary that she couldn't face it—elementary like...love?

She closed her eyes and her mind to the conversation. She needed sleep to get better, to gain her strength of mind and body back. Sam and the problems he caused could wait until another day.

She rolled over and dreamed of Sam, his arms around her, his smile shining on her like the warm sun. They were looking at children at play, their children, and he was so proud.

And so was she. Her children would never know what it was like to have childhood taken from them, snatched like a thief in the night. They would have a normal life. Her children would love and be loved. They would play dress up and march in parades, just like the children she had seen today and envied. Her children with the dark hair and big brown eyes and the tall athletic build of their father...her children would be happy and carefree and wonderful....

8

CATHERINE AWOKE to the banging of pots and pans. She listened for a moment, attempting to orient herself. Then she realized she was in Sam's house and he was probably in the kitchen making breakfast.

She wondered why he wasn't at work. He had come home early yesterday but he hadn't said why, and she'd been so happy to see him that she hadn't questioned him.

She jumped out of bed and dashed into the bathroom, quietly closing the door behind her. She quickly ran a washcloth over her face, brushed her teeth with one of Sam's hated toothbrushes and slipped into her shorts and top from yesterday. Her stomach gave a loud growl. Coffee and toast were the order of the moment.

Sam's lightly breathed cursing was filling the air as she walked into the kitchen. A hand rubbing his head told the story.

She chuckled. "Hit your head?"

He glowered accusingly at the pots that dangled on brass hooks suspended from the ceiling and arrowed down toward the butcher block in the middle of the kitchen. "These damn things are out to get me. I need to move those chains so I don't get bumped every time I turn around."

"You do that and no one will be able to reach anything except you and the Jolly Green Giant."

He grinned. "Do I seem that tall to you?"

She grinned back, not thinking through her answer before giving it. "No, you're just right." At his surprised look, she quickly added, "For your pots and pans to wreak vengeance on the one who puts them to work most often."

"Thanks," he muttered. "By the way, put on a bathing suit and grab a few towels. We're going to the beach today." He paused. "Er, that is, do you like the beach? Would you like to go?"

Her eyes grew wide with delight. "I'd love to! I've never been before."

"Never?" His look was incredulous. "You grew up in New Orleans and never walked down to the beach?"

"I grew up around the docks, and the beach was a long way away," she corrected. "I always wanted to, but there was too much else to do."

He looked skeptical, but didn't ask the questions that seemed poised on his tongue. He couldn't imagine any teenager living near a beach and never going there. Turning away he poured another cup of coffee, then handed it to her. "Well, get ready for a fun experience."

She gratefully sipped on the coffee, wondering what could be so wonderful about a tour of a beach. One glance at the look that blazed from his eyes and she knew not to ask.

With Sam Lewis, One Hour at a Time was fast becoming her motto.

"Two perfect days in a row," Sam murmured contentedly as he pulled into the beach parking lot. "California is nothing if not full of surprises."

The car came to a stop and Catherine slipped out,

anxious to feel the salty wind. She took several deep breaths, losing the inhibitions that had tethered her this past week. Today was not the time to worry about the future. She had the rest of her life to do that. All she wanted to do was enjoy herself, enjoy Sam's company and enjoy the beach.

Sam pointed toward the old remains of a pier, then burrowed into the trunk of the car. "Head over there. I'll follow behind."

"Why? I'll wait for you." She turned, hands outstretched to carry some of the things he had decided were a necessity to this trip. He plopped blankets and towels in her open arms.

"Because I'm in charge of this expedition and I say I get to watch the scenery as I walk. It's only fair."

"The scenery...?" She grinned beguilingly. "In that case, I have the same option."

"No, you don't. You've never seen the beach so you fill your eyes with that view. On the other hand, I've seen the beach plenty of times, so I get the view of my choice, and my choice is watching you walk."

She dimpled saucily. "Enjoy yourself," she caroled, strutting ahead toward the spot he had pointed to earlier. She couldn't help the extra swing she put in her walk, she felt buoyant with fun and freedom. Sam gave a mock growl, which only made her giggle and wiggle her hips more.

He had chosen a spot by an old, drunkenly-tilted pier beam and close to the ocean's edge. It was away from the crowd and she was glad. Sam was enough to deal with. Blankets were spread, towels divided and a picnic basket set to the side before they stripped off T-shirts and jeans to worship the sun in their bathing suits.

Catherine's was a royal-blue two-piece that was far more modest than most on the beach. Sam wore a black knit that would have been more at home on the beaches of Europe. It showed everything, and he didn't seem to mind at all. Silently, Catherine agreed with him. She didn't mind, either.

"It's a wonder you're not attacked by every female within a hundred yards," she muttered in a voice she hoped was unappreciative of his looks.

His brown eyes twinkled. "Does that apply to you, too?"

"Forget it. When the game is obviously a win, the hunter moves on to more elusive game."

"Oh, Lord," he groaned, and she chuckled.

"Bad, huh?" she asked.

"Bad," he confirmed.

She shrugged, turning her back to him as she began rubbing suntan lotion on her legs and arms.

"Can I help?" His stomach was tightening again. She not only had the sweetest little derriere, but her back was soft and smooth and so beautifully sculptured.

"No, thanks." Her voice was muffled and soft, rasping along his nerves to tighten them even more.

He watched like a hungry man dying for sustenance as her long, tapered fingers swept over the very areas he would have loved to have caressed. His palms itched with every stroke. Her fingers massaged, they curved, then stroked, and he felt every curve, every indentation she touched. Not only was her skin beautiful and soft, but the oil made it delightfully sensuous and slippery. He could imagine his hand slipping to her stomach, then following the oiled path downward. . . .

Finally, breathing shallowly and berating himself for

being a masochist, he lay on his back and allowed the sun's rays to temporarily blind him. With his eyes closed he could still feel her nearness, and his body continued to react to her. When she scooted around, he heard her soft gasp and knew that she had seen the evidence of his arousal. It satisfied him. Let her know that she was the cause of his discomfort, it served her right.

Instead, all he heard was a very undignified, slightly muffled chuckle, which left a small quirk of a smile on his mouth. He should have known the situation would backfire.

Catherine leaned back and closed her eyes, mimicking Sam. It was heavenly. The sun seemed to seep into her very pores, and the sound of the softly lapping waves was almost mesmerizing. She was content. She knew that even with her eyes closed she could reach out and Sam would be there, next to her, and that feeling gave her another sense of peace. One she hadn't had in a long time. With that thought, she drifted into a light sleep.

Something tickled her upper lip, teasing it into puckering. She opened her mouth and stuck out her tongue, coming into contact with something crusty and good smelling. Fried chicken. Her white teeth held on and grabbed a bite, not letting go until she had a healthy portion in her mouth. "Mmm."

"I thought you'd like that," Sam's low voice teased her, washing over her with the same feeling that the day had given her, relaxed and slightly daring.

"I loved it," she said with her eyes still closed. "Is there more where that came from?"

"Yes, and just as tasty."

Her brows rose over lidded eyes. "Tasty, yes, but what about crisp?"

"And crisp," he said, almost in a whisper. "And warm. And waiting for you."

"The perfect meal."

"For you, maybe. My appetite runs to other. . .delicacies." He cleared his throat, forcibly willing his mind back to safer ground.

"Can I have some more, please?"

"You bet. Only sit up before the sun fries *you* to a crisp." He sounded gruff to his own ears, but he couldn't help it.

She did as she was told and he handed her the drumstick. She chewed hungrily, finishing it in nothing flat.

Sam glanced away, staring at the ocean instead of Catherine until he felt more in control. The effort it took him to slow down his heartbeat almost exhausted him. But finally, he was able to take a deep breath and look at her without feeling like a hungry, slavering wolf. "Cold drink?"

"Please." And she drank it down quickly.

"If I'd known this was to be a marathon, I'd have entered the race," Sam said dryly.

"Listen," Catherine put in as she leaned back on her elbows enjoying the heat of the sun playing upon her body. "This sunbathing is hard work. It takes more muscle control being still than it does working."

"So I gather. Do you always work so hard?"

Suddenly the teasing left her voice. "I've had to. No one works for you, or haven't you noticed?" She laid back down so that she didn't have to face him. Her eyes were closed, her ears concentrating on the sound of the surf.

Suddenly his shadow fell across her, blocking the sun's rays, and she felt the change in temperature immediately. Her eyes opened just a little to see him watching her with narrowed eyes, searching her face for something, but she didn't know what.

"You're beautiful, do you know that?"

"I think I might have heard it once or twice before." Poor Sam. He was darling but he sure wasn't original.

"No, I mean beautiful. Both inside and out."

Her brows rose. "How would you know? You hardly know me."

"I know more than you think, Catherine. I know you seem to have an inferiority complex as big as the Pacific Ocean. I know you feel guilty at times, but I'm not sure why. I know you have an honest sense of fair play or you wouldn't have tried to reassure April of your relationship with Jace. I know that you try hard at everything you do, giving it your best whether it's sunbathing or cooking or reading a book."

"My, my, the attorney at work."

He smiled and her heart skipped a beat with the beauty of it. His head came down, ever so slowly, his lips barely touching hers. "No work today. Just play. I'd like to play with you, Catherine Sinclair, except that I'm not sure you know the rules of the game."

"To the victor goes the spoils?" Her voice was clipped, but breathless.

"No. Winner takes all and there are no losers." His lips took hers then, and the sun was blocked by his head, making her feel both hot and cold at the same time. Only it was reversed. Where the sun blazed down she was hot on the outside but cool on the inside, and where Sam shielded her body from the sun, she was cool on the outside and hot on the inside. She felt all soft and warm and melting. Her arms came up to circle his neck, only to stop at his nape and feel the texture of his hair in the palm of her hand. It felt so strong and fresh and vital.

His tongue probed hers, and she answered with her own soft thrusts, willing him to take more, to see if he could absorb her into him so that she'd be a part of him. A child cried and a mother soothed, a man yelled at his son, a radio blared out rock music, but it was all far away. It melded with sounds of ocean and breathing and needs and wants.

Then he pulled back and her mouth missed him. His lips strayed to the top of her breast and she sucked in the hot, salty air. One tanned finger pushed away the scrap of blue material that covered her nipple and before she could respond, his teeth and lips and tongue had captured it, sending even deeper spirals of heat surging through her. Her hands tightened on his shoulders as she arched to give him better access and he accommodated himself to her, knowing his body blocked the view.

When she thought she could take no more, Sam's mouth left her breast to travel back to her lips, giving small nips on the way. One hand teased the edge of her bikini pants, fingers slipping under the material to spread whatever oil was left on her skin.

A moan echoed in her throat to vibrate against his mouth. He drew away and took several deep breaths, resting his head against the curve of her shoulder.

Finally he spoke. "I want you, Catherine, you know that. I want to see you wearing nothing but nature, air soothing your body, light shimmering against your skin." He took another breath, then quickly replaced the bit of cloth over her breast. "But not here."

Her voice shook as she answered. "Why not? We could sell tickets and have an audience in no time."

"That's exactly what I'm afraid of," he muttered. "And I won't share you with anyone. But if I keep it up I won't be able to stop, and that scares me even more."

"How can you talk about something that scares you, Sam?" He had pulled away, but his tobacco-brown eyes wouldn't allow her gaze to stray.

"Because when I talk about it, it becomes smaller than it really is. It's only when I keep it to myself that things grow until I can't control them."

She smiled but it was tinged with sadness. "Is this a paid commercial announcement?"

Still his eyes were locked with hers. "Yes."

"Thank you for trying to help."

"I'm here, Catherine. Whenever. I'm here."

Her hand came up to stroke his jaw, resting there to quiver with the wonder of wanting him and the joy of being with him. "I know," she whispered. "I know."

They passed the rest of the day in glib conversation, both hiding their private emotions behind easy answers and quick retorts. Catherine knew it couldn't last, but she didn't care right now. She needed a friend, and Sam was it.

They walked away from the crowds and toward the private homes scattered among the sand dunes. They collected seashells of various colors and sizes, Catherine washing them off carefully in the waves before wrapping them in the saran wrap that had held a part of their lunch. They slowly strolled along, holding hands and staring straight ahead as if they were simply friends.

Just the way she wanted it.

Sam broke the long, easy silence. "I wish I could say

I'm sorry things didn't work out for you and Jace, but I'd be lying," he confessed haltingly. "April and Jace are too good together. Besides, then I wouldn't be walking along the beach with you."

Catherine bent to pick up a shell. "But things did work out for Jace and me."

Sam stopped. "I don't understand." A frown marred his brow.

She smiled as if she were talking to a child. "He and I were good friends. We both made it in the profession of our choice, as they say, and we are both still friends. What more could we ask for?"

His confused expression told Catherine more than anything he said. "But I thought, that is, when I spoke to you after the party . . ."

The joy left her blue eyes momentarily. "You thought I was talking about Jace?"

He nodded, his hands resting lightly on her shoulders as they stood, wrapped in their own world.

"No." She shook her head slowly as if to emphasize her point. "It was someone else I was talking about. I thought you knew."

A gull screamed overhead. Sam's expression changed from one of confusion to dawning comprehension. Noah Weston. "I do, now," he said softly.

They began walking the beach again, hand in hand. "So you and Jace were just good friends?" he asked with what he hoped was a casual tone.

Catherine chuckled, sending a delightful chill down his spine. "We were friends as only two people can be when they both feel they're in the same boat. Neither one of us were getting ahead in our chosen professions and didn't know what we were going to do about it. He was just beginning in movies and didn't really know what direction he wanted to go—director, actor, producer. And I was cleaning ashtrays in a recording studio and using the bands' leftover time to hone my craft."

"Leftover time?"

"Yes. Sometimes someone will pay for a set amount of studio time—one, two or three hours—to cut a tape of themselves. If they finish early, then they'll sell the rest of the band's time for a lower than usual rate. I used to save pennies to buy that time and cut my own tapes."

"What did you do with the tapes?"

"I sent them to every disc jockey in the country hoping one of them would play it on the air and say, 'That's a great new singer, folks! Run out and ask for her album!'"

"And did that happen, Catherine?" His brown eyes stared down at her, showing the respect he had for her persistence.

She grinned. "Never. But then a man came in to view the studio for investment purposes. When I heard about it I slipped into the control room and ran my tape through the P.A. system. He heard every song I ever taped in the space of three hours." She chuckled at her remembered audacity. "It was kind of like a Catherine Sinclair marathon."

The papers had lauded her from state to state when she had her first hit song. The newspapers couldn't get enough information about her. One man was supposedly responsible for her success.

"Noah Weston," Sam said quietly.

"Yes." Her voice was as low as his.

"So you were trying to become a singer *before* he met you, not *because* he met you."

"Yes."

Sam stopped, turning her toward him and grasping hold of both her hands. The surf gently rocked against the sand, making a soft shushing sound. A gull landed at their feet, picking away at crumbs others had left.

"So the hype the newspapers built up wasn't exactly true."

"No. Hardly any of it is true. But it made sensational copy, sold newspapers and magazines, and got my name in front of the public, so it worked." Her eyes locked with his. The force of his feelings were being transmitted through his hands. She could feel herself growing stronger, becoming more tense, wanting whatever he wanted. . . .

His eyes narrowed, making delightful crow's-feet at the corners. "Do you realize, you're probably the only person who knows who you really are?"

He was hitting very close to home, but she couldn't resist teasing. She nodded her head. "And I'm not telling." She couldn't admit that even she wasn't sure of her own identity. Only with Sam did the two halves of her seem to come together peacefully.

His brows rose, his hands tightened around hers, one thumb placing itself smack in the center of her palm and pressing just enough to let her know her own softness. "Not even to me? I'm supposed to be a friend."

"A touchy friend," she put in.

"All friends touch. You know what I mean. Stop with the puns."

"Oh, ho, we're supposed to be serious, too? I thought this was my day at the beach to relax and enjoy, not go into therapy."

He gave her hands a shake. "You're supposed to be straight with friends and lawyers. It's in the books."

The ghost of a smile she had been wearing disappeared. "And you're supposed to believe that your client is innocent until proven guilty. But you had already judged me, hadn't you, Sam?"

"Don't be silly! I knew from the beginning that you hadn't stolen that necklace!" Sam flipped his hair away from his forehead, impatience lacing his movements.

"No, not about the necklace. About the type of woman I was supposed to be. You believed the publicity."

"No." His voice was so soft it was almost carried away by the salt-scented breeze. "I never did."

Catherine pulled her hands from his and turned to walk the shoreline again. Her bare feet scuffed at the wet sand, her head down to watch her steps. "Why, Sam? I can't make heads or tails out of you. You say you won't help, then you come to my rescue. You hold me all night without one sexy move. You have me move in with you, then you make love to me as if you hadn't seen a woman in years. Then you say you want to be friends and you act like a lover. What is it with you?" She stopped to face him, her eyes showing the deep confusion she felt. He had turned her life upside down. He had turned *her* upside down.

Sam was lost in the blue of her eyes, falling down into heavens unknown to him until she'd walked into his life. His hands wanted to touch, to seek, to ensure she was real. But he couldn't reach out to her, and he knew it.

"I don't know," he said slowly, his voice roughened by desire. "But I know that the way I behaved was what I needed to do or say at that moment. I can't explain it. I'm not even sure it makes sense to me."

She continued to look directly at him, the honesty of her gaze making him tremble inside. "Can we be friends, Sam? Is it really possible?"

Finally he reached out to touch her. His hand rested on her shoulder and turned her toward the ocean waves that lapped at their feet. He brought her back close to his chest so he could feel the softness of her as they both stared out at the vast emptiness of seascape. His lips grazed her temple in a whisper of a kiss. "I don't know, but I sure want to try."

She gave a small sigh and her hair blew to caress his shoulder. "Then we'll try, Sam," she said slowly. "I could use a friend." She had finally admitted it, and the admission felt good. . . right.

The sun blazed from a bright lemon color to a brilliant orange ball as Catherine and Sam walked hand in hand back to the pier where their blanket was. They kept silent, for it was companionable and easy, only Sam's mind was going one hundred miles an hour. Catherine needed more than a friend, but she didn't know it yet.

Catherine needed him. For a long, long time.

THEY ATE DINNER at a trendy little spot not far from the beach, where casual attire was the rule. Fishnets filled with an assortment of seashells hung from the rough-hewn rafters, while the tables were slick and clear and displayed a closer view of similar shells. The seafood was excellent, the wine and iced tea crisp and cold to the palate, and the conversation was light.

Sam leaned back, sipping his wine in the hopes that it would calm the butterflies in his stomach. In a little while this magic interlude would be over, and they would head for home. Then they would be completely alone. Was she worried that he would ask her to his bed? Was he afraid she would refuse? Probably a "yes" for her and a definite "yes" for him.

Catherine sipped her tea, closing her eyes in enjoyment. It had been a near-perfect day.

"How was your first experience at the beach?" he asked in an easy tone.

Her eyes opened to stare directly at him. "I loved it. Thank you."

"For the beach? It's always been there, I had nothing to do with it."

She smiled and his heart did a flip-flop. "For taking me."

He dipped his head and smiled in return, unable to do anything else. "My pleasure. Anytime, my lady."

Her eyes twinkled. "In that case, we'll go tomorrow and the next day, and the next day, and the—"

He saw the error of his ways. "Anytime I can get away from work, which is usually a weekend," he corrected quickly.

Her eyes grew wide in innocence. "Oh," she said as if it were a disappointment. His heart did another flip-flop. He wished he could give her her heart's desires, even though he knew better than to think it.

Then he saw the twinkle in her eyes and his day lightened again. "In that case," she said in a teasing voice, "I'm buying that painting right above your head." She pointed to a seascape with an artist's card and amount in the bottom left-hand corner.

Sam craned to see it. It wasn't bad as far as seascapes went, but it was a little on the commercial side. The price was definitely inflated. "I don't think it's worth the amount he's asking, Catherine."

She stiffened right before his eyes. The enjoyment on her face had evaporated to show the strength of conviction of the woman underneath the feminine doll-like exterior. "Does it matter? I like it."

He raised his hand in the air as if to stop her from saying anymore. "Hey, it's your money, lady, not mine. You can buy the Taj Mahal if it suits you."

"Thank you."

"But the dinner bill is mine," he muttered between clenched teeth. Leave it to him to fall in love with a women's libber! Brenda would say it was only justice, but he thought it was the pits.

As if she could read his mind, she tried to mollify him. "I want to thank you for a delicious lunch and dinner," she said softly.

His grin was reluctantly given. "You're welcome. Did you say that because you really enjoyed it, or because your mama taught you to be mannerly?"

Again he lost her. The softness was gone. "My 'mama' didn't teach me a damn thing I could do in public. . . . I learned it all on my own."

Sam stared down at his wine, then back up at Catherine. He should have known better than to mention the very subject he knew would close her up. "One more strike and I'll be out of the ball park. I'm sorry, I was only joking."

Catherine waved to the waitress to get her attention. "I wish I was," she clipped.

They were ready to leave, bill paid and painting under Catherine's arm, in less than ten minutes. The tension was strung so tight it was almost visible.

The drive home was the longest one Sam had ever taken, or so it seemed. Fifteen minutes ago had he really been contemplating about their making love when they got home? He must have been insane. Not only that, he must have rocks in his head for falling in love with a woman who changed from warm to chilling in less than a second.

Damn Catherine Sinclair! He didn't need her, she needed him. He didn't need another thing—his life was nice and quiet and orderly without her. His days and nights were filled with a routine that he could count on...boring, repetitious. His spine stiffened. And that was the way it would be again, he promised himself. In another week or so the necklace business would be taken care of, and Catherine would be out of his life completely. He might be lonely at first, but he'd be a better man for it. Better for what, he wasn't sure, but at least it'd be better than this roller coaster his emotions had been riding since she entered his life. He hadn't been this befuddled since he had been a green recruit in the military, years ago! But he had made it through that and he would make it through this.

Somehow that little pep talk made him feel better, even though he knew he was lying to himself.

This too would pass, and he could chalk it up to one of life's learning experiences.

By the time they had showered and readied for bed, both in their own separate bedrooms, Sam was more tense than he'd been in the restaurant. She was one thin wall away from him: thirty steps if he took the hallway. And he couldn't move off the bed to go to her.

He fluffed and propped the pillows against the headboard and leaned back, his arms behind his head. Then he tried to bore a hole in the wall in front of him. He could almost see her moving around on the other side of the wall. The shower had stopped a few minutes ago. He could picture her pulling the towel off her body and slipping into a sheer, sexy nightgown. He heard her rummage through her suitcase and wondered what she was looking for. Panties? Hairbrush? Dainty slippers? He ruled out the panties—she hardly wore them when she was dressed so he doubted that she would wear them to bed. Slippers didn't fit either. She always seemed to wander around barefoot. It must be the hairbrush. She was probably running it through her light-blond hair right now. He counted the strokes and with each stroke his body tightened. Fifty, fifty-one, fifty-two...

THE COARSE SAND had acted as an abrasive against Catherine's skin. She applied a generous amount of lotion to her legs and began rubbing. Thoughts best left alone came forward to haunt her. Her hands became Sam's and she watched without watching as they stroked her skin so firmly but gently. He was only one thin wall away.

Somehow she knew that Sam would not come to her. If anything were going to happen between them, it would have to be instigated by her. And she couldn't do that.

She had never gone after any man. Even Noah had singled her out, not the other way around. And only when she thought she was in love with him had she lost inhibitions enough to damage both of them. Never again.

She took another dollop of cream and began rubbing it into her arms. But the feelings she experienced with Sam were very different from those she'd had with Noah.

Noah—a chapter in her life that was over, and she desperately wished the embarrassment would go with it. She had paid for that folly a thousand times, in both guilt and reputation. She had tried to hold on to him and to all he represented for too long, and had made a fool of herself in the bargain.

But Sam...Sam was different. She not only felt safe and secure with him, she *liked* him. He was fun and witty and tender and boyish and...vulnerable.

Her hand stopped massaging. Vulnerable, what an odd word, but it fit him. She felt unprotected, too, but she had built a wall that she didn't think anyone could ever knock down, while he allowed others to see his vulnerability. And in doing so, he had become an enigma to her.

She wiped her hands on a towel and picked up her hairbrush. Stroke, stroke, stroke; she forgot to keep count as she stared at the painting propped on the dresser.

Any other man would have offered to buy the seascape for her, but not Sam. If she wanted it, she could have it, but she had to pay for it. She grinned. She *would* have to be attached to a man who believed in women's lib!

With a small sigh, she placed the brush on the nightstand and turned out the light. Slipping under the covers, she closed her eyes and willed herself to sleep.

It was no use. She wanted Sam near her. She longed to feel the heat of his body radiating under the covers, his legs just inches away from hers. She wanted to rest her head on his broad chest and feel his arms around her, his heartbeat in her ear. She wanted her hand tucked into his for comfort.

She wanted Sam. Now. Tonight. And hang the damn codes that expected her to wait for him to make the move! With her luck he would never ask her to his bed and she'd be lonely forever.

What was that old expression? Oh, yes. Woman chooses the man who will choose her. That thought brought Catherine to a sitting position. She'd always acted contrary to what was expected. But perhaps that expression was right, and she wanted Sam because he had so expertly chased her. No, that wasn't the reason. He was everything she had ever wanted in a man. He was her perfect choice for a partner. . . .

She knew what her thoughts were telling her, but she hated to admit that she cared more than she promised herself she would.

But as long as he didn't know how much she cared for him, would it hurt? Of course not.

Her feet almost flew across the carpet toward the door. Her hand didn't hesitate on the knob; she opened the door swiftly and went out into the hall. She stopped just in front of his door.

He was on the other side. Would he send her away? Would he be angry with her? Would he care one way or the other? "Cowardice gets you nothing, girl. Didn't you teach yourself that years ago?" she silently muttered. Then she stood straight. She was Catherine Sinclair, the singer, the beauty with the wild reputation. Any man would do cartwheels to go to bed with her! Sam couldn't be *that* different from other men! Courage!

SAM'S EYES were still glued to the wall when he heard the door to his room give a reluctant but loud squeak. He didn't move a muscle except to switch his eyes to the door. The view made his breathing stop even though his pulse quickened in hunger.

Catherine stood in the darkened hallway, her shimmering pale-green nightgown doing crazy things to him. Her hair was down and straight, making her look like Alice in Wonderland, but her shapely body was definitely that of a grown woman. He waited for her to say something so he would know why she was here, how to respond, what to do. His usually computerlike mind refused to function without her input.

Her hands came up only to fall helplessly at her sides, a graceful motion that resembled the soft movements of a butterfly.

"Sam, I . . ."

With blinding insight he knew exactly what to do.

He held out his arms and she flew into them.

9

THE DULL, FALSE BEGINNING of morning light slowly filtered through the window. Catherine moved, stretching gingerly. When she encountered a male leg, Sam's leg, she halted, opening her eyes to look up at the man next to her. His eyes were wide open, his mouth forming a small, delicious smile of contentment.

Without a word he reached for her, one large hand cupping a breast, softly teasing the flesh with whisper like touches. She turned toward him, leaning on her side to make access to his broad chest easier for herself. Her fingers traced the crisp mat of hair, finally mimicking his movements as she teased his flat male nipple into a small nub of hardness, staring into his eyes all the while.

When his hand left her breast to travel leisurely down the flatness of her stomach and beyond, she did the same.

His breath caught in his throat.

His hand dipped lower still, finding the warmth he had been seeking, plying her with gentle caresses that made her temperature soar. Her breath came lightly, quickly, almost whistling in her throat, matching the cadence of his.

Then her mouth came forward and she teased the tip of his nipple with her tongue, leaving a heated coolness there. Her small white teeth nipped the edge of a rib, touched further down his ribcage, then traveled to his navel to tease him even more. She was the amazon, the aggressor, the woman who made the moves. It was a heady power.

Sam's control was slipping away, his eyes filling with need. His touch became more rapid, less than gentle. He tried to reach places that he had to caress to feel her response and couldn't do so. She wouldn't let him. She was controlling the situation and he had no choice but to follow. Frustration added to the need that was building into a tightly wound coil deep inside him.

Her head went further down still, giving him a kiss that only the closest of lovers could give. A deep, gravelly moan forced its way past his lips. His hands cradled the head that tried so sweetly to please him, his fingers tangling in the blond hair that spilled across his stomach and thighs.

Suddenly the tension was too much and with hands that shook he raised her to his level, his lips and tongue taking hers in a searing kiss that lit fires where none had been before. As his kiss deepened and their tongues dueled for supremacy, he turned so that she was beneath him, rocking against his hips in silent supplication.

But he wasn't ready to soothe her needs. Not yet. Two could play her game and he meant to follow her lead.

His lips touched her neck, then trailed downward until he found her budding nipple. He toyed with her, making her squirm with desire as he teased first one rigid peak and then the other. His hands squeezed her waist, his head moving even lower until he found her small navel. His tongue dipped, then foraged on, leaving a damp heat everywhere he touched.

Suddenly his mouth was at the most intimate of places, feeding fire and ice into the very core of her soul. His tongue sought her very desire, urging her on to levels of tormenting ecstasy she had never known before. She arched, attempting to pull away, but his hands held her locked to him. A moan seared her throat but her mouth couldn't form the words that would stop him. Her mind ceased to function. Her hands clenched his shoulders, telling him with action what she wanted.

Then he was there, in her and filling her with mutual need. This time they each heard the other's voice. They sought lips that could give as well as take, and in a final burst of passion, they became one.

"My Kitty, my Catherine," Sam murmured against her shoulder, accepting that the two personalities of her had merged together in their lovemaking. His kisses were sweet, gentle, tender, telling her how much he had been touched by their morning passion.

All she could do was smile and stroke his back and shoulders, reveling in the feeling of the blanket of weight he was on her. He was here, with her, touching her, and his touching was healing. A balm that made old hurts disappear as if by magic.

A single emotion bloomed forth but she was too tired to put it into words. She hugged his body close, tightened her grip, then let go, her body and mind exhausted from the gamut of experience he had just given her. It was too much for her to absorb. With a feeling of complete contentment she had never felt before, she gave a sigh and slipped into a deep sleep.

She woke several hours later, her heart light with feelings that were best left unexpressed for fear the source of her happiness would disappear. After getting the morning paper from the lawn, she made a full pot of coffee and almost half a loaf of toast, then carried it back to the bedroom on a tray.

They drank coffee, ate toast and argued about the news, a friendly banter that continued well into the morning. No mention was made of the night before and Catherine's returning to his bed and his arms. It was as if the subject were taboo for both of them. It was a magical time, the world outside their front door didn't exist. As time sped toward Sam's luncheon appointment with his friend and fellow attorney, Leo Coulter, the more reluctant he became to leave Catherine.

That was stupid, his conscience told him. After all, she was a grown woman and certainly didn't need a babysitter. But he knew the real reason. He loved being around her. She was like a refreshing tonic to him, and he couldn't seem to get enough to drink.

However he had been sane at his office Monday and had cancelled everything but this luncheon with Leo. When he was around Catherine he couldn't think straight. He needed time to get away, put his thoughts in order and decide on a course of action. What exactly that meant, he didn't know. He just knew that he needed to give them both a little time away from each other.

The wisdom of his luncheon was brought home to him when she asked him if he liked chocolate and mentioned something about a cake recipe she wanted to try. He knew that he either had to go to his luncheon or sit like a star-struck teenager and watch her bake. He chose the luncheon.

He met Leo in an intimate French restaurant not far from his office. Sam had known Leo at law school. They had found a special friendship growing between them, probably because they were two of a kind. Both had bummed around a long time before settling on a career choice, both had worked while attending school in order to afford the tuition. Only recently had the two of them begun to enjoy life and appreciate the finer things they had only dreamed about before. They had one other thing in common: they both loved women. All of them.

"You don't look any worse for wear," Sam said as he took the seat across from Leo. Because of his friend's large muscular build and striking hazel eyes, he commanded immediate attention everywhere he went, especially in the courtroom. Men thought his light-eyed stare was cold, but women seemed to swoon over it. That, along with his dark brows made a marked contrast to his casually windswept blond hair. In anybody's book, Leo was handsome.

"If you're referring to that long legged redhead, then I'll confess. She's too much for me."

Sam's brows shot up. "I don't believe it! You're crying uncle after the intensive search and seizure technique you put her through?"

"I found out that she had her own techniques, and I'm not sure I cared to be the hunted."

Sam chuckled. "You mean marriage?"

Leo joined him, a deep rumble that shook his broad shoulders. "Marriage, love and babies. She wanted it all and wouldn't mind cheating just a bit to get her way."

"But don't you think it's about time you settled down?" Sam asked as he watched the waiter pour a cool, white wine into his glass. Leo had obviously gotten impatient and ordered the wine for both of them. He wondered who he was addressing the question to, himself or Leo.

"With a woman who wants me...or my money?" Leo said dryly. "I don't seem to have any problem attracting the latter, but it's the former that makes the best wife."

Sam leaned back, smiling. "I should have known you'd have all the answers. But someday someone is going to conk you right over your hard head and drag you home to her cave. You won't stand a chance, buddy." He couldn't help the smile that still framed his mouth. Ages ago both April and Jace had met Leo. Jace had thought him to be a caveman while April likened him to a huge tan-and-gold teddy bear. Either description fit him.

"Maybe not, but I'll put up one hell of a fight until I'm dragged through the door."

They ordered, then sat back and talked shop, both touching bases with their own lives.

Then, slowly, Sam returned to the original conversation. "Leo, what would you say if I told you I was in love?"

"I'd say you're crazy and the only cure I know is to move in with her for a while. It always eases the pain of separation when I've had to put up with togetherness for any length of time."

Sam stared at his veal. "And what if that doesn't work?"

"Then you're hooked, man. I only hope she's good enough for you." Leo shook his head as if he had just heard about a good friend's funeral. "Does she feel the same way, I hope?"

"If she does, it's a carefully guarded secret. She cares, but I don't think she loves."

Leo leaned forward, his expression showing Sam just

how sincere he was. "Then cut it off, man. It's not worth the agony you'll go through if you let it continue."

"And who hurt you?" Sam's voice was caustic with the anger he felt toward his friend for voicing what Sam wouldn't even think.

"What else? A woman. She was my wife for exactly one year, then everything went down the drain. I suffered for years before I came to terms with it and decided that from then on, my heart would stay where it belonged... in my chest."

"Too late," Sam said in a growl. "Your advice is just too late."

"Who is she, and what does she want?" Leo asked as he cut into his meal. Nothing seemed to stop Leo from eating. Nothing.

Slowly, almost haltingly, Sam told Leo about Catherine. He left out nothing except their sweet loving. That was no one's business.

Leo leaned back, for once shocked enough not to lift his fork for a few minutes. "Wow. You are in deep trouble, my man. You are already sunk."

Sam shrugged his shoulders, unwilling to admit that Leo was probably right. But the diamond-hard gleam in his eyes seemed to say that he wasn't going to lose Catherine without a fight.

"What about the thief? Any leads?"

Sam nodded, cautiously reticent. "A few. I hired a private investigator two days ago. He's given me some information and has a crew watching her house around the clock. They're changing the locks but they still expect the burglar to return."

"Any suspects?"

"None yet," Sam hedged, thinking of the phone call

he had made earlier to the private investigating firm. They had a lead but Sam didn't know if it was the right one or not. Time would tell.

Leo lifted his glass. "I toast you and your efforts, Sam. From what little I know about Catherine Sinclair, she has the ambition of ten, no a hundred women. She certainly wouldn't entertain the notion of falling for a man who isn't the next Perry Mason any more than she would fall for a country doctor when she could have De Bakey." Leo took a deep breath and continued, "You, my friend, don't have enough ambition for her kind. You'd either have to change or be run into the ground by her nagging. There isn't a chance in a thousand for this romance to succeed."

"I appreciate your opinion, but you'll understand if I don't believe it." Sam's voice was hard but his mind was spinning. Of all the many reasons he knew were against their relationship succeeding, he had never thought of Leo's. "Besides, she knows that I'm happy with what I'm doing."

"Does she? Really?" Leo looked skeptical.

"Yes," Sam ground out. Visions of last night flitted through his mind. She had come to him. Did she care and just not know it? Could she care and not show it? No, that didn't make sense.

"Well, I wish you luck. But I personally think you're out of your mind. And your league. And your depth."

"Thanks for nothing, Leo." Sam stood and took out his wallet. "I come here hoping for some moral support and you hand me negatives. I'll remember it, buddy, when the next redhead pops into your life and you need to talk out your strategy." He threw the bills on the table. "See you later," he muttered, leaving the restaurant.

He needed to be home. With Catherine. Now.

Once more he opened his front door to smell the savory aromas that proclaimed a sinfully delicious home-cooked meal. And once more Catherine peeked from the kitchen, her hair in a ponytail that made her look all of sixteen, her body encased in a lightweight, cream-colored sweater and royal-blue slacks that proved she was all woman.

"I hope you like early dinners," she called from the kitchen as she disappeared behind the door. "'Cause that's what you're getting."

He cleared the lump in his throat. "That's fine with me."

"Good. Then we won't have to cook this evening. We'll nibble on leftovers and enjoy the lack of mess."

He stood in the kitchen doorway and watched her stir something in one of the pots. She looked completely at home, contented and in her element. Could Catherine really dislike him for what Leo thought was his lack of ambition? He stood straighter. It didn't matter. He was what he was and loved his work.

He walked to the counter and picked up the blender, then headed toward the refrigerator for ice. "Want a margarita?" he asked over his shoulder.

"Mmm, thanks. But without the liquor, please."

With deft movements he made quick work of two drinks, one with and one without.

Handing Catherine her drink, he almost downed his own in one swallow. The slushy ice nearly froze his throat, then his stomach. But it took away the pain that seemed to surround his heart when he was with her.

She took a sip, watching him carefully. "I think we ought to make a toast," she said.

"Oh?" he managed to get out. "To what?"

"To friendship." She raised her glass and tapped it against his before taking another sip. He dutifully lifted his and drank the very last drop.

"Now let's eat," he said gruffly, ignoring the fullness of his stomach from his lunch with Leo. "We have those insurance papers to complete, and then I have some work to do here at home."

Confusion once more lit her bright-blue eyes. "Okay."

"Catherine," he said abruptly, then halted, only to begin again. "Catherine, I love my work. It pays well although I'll never be a millionaire, but the satisfaction I receive is tremendous. I wouldn't change it for the world. Do you understand that?"

She ran her finger around the rim, one part of her mind on him while the other wondered how he could drink the horrible stuff he just concocted. She looked up. "Is it important?"

"Yes," he snapped.

"Then I understand."

He waited a minute, then nodded his head. "Good," he said and walked out of the room.

Catherine once more stirred the steaming vegetables. And men said women's thoughts were hard to follow!

THEY ATE DINNER in silence. Afterward they cleaned the kitchen. Then they sat at Sam's desk in his den and quietly filled out the insurance papers. Only necessary questions were asked and only the shortest of answers were given.

Sam walked six blocks to the nearest mailbox, trying to work off his mood. But his frustration level continued to climb. He wanted this woman for all the wrong reasons, knowing she couldn't be his no matter how much he craved her. Last night and this morning, when he had held her close and smelled the perfume of her body, felt the softness of her skin, she was his. But after dawn came, so did reality.

Damn reality!

He jammed the letter into the box and slammed the lid. Blast everything! She was his! It was just a matter of convincing her of the fact, that was all.

He slowly smiled. And he had the rest of the week in which to do it.

WHEN JACE CALLED on Thursday to ask them to a new club opening, Sam jumped at the chance. It was just what he and Catherine needed—a change of scene. Since their first date and Sam's misunderstanding, Jace had been a silent bone of contention between them, and this would be the perfect opportunity to lay those feelings to rest. It was a test, a small one, but just one of many to come.

Catherine, too, was pleased at the invitation, which pained Sam more than he was willing to admit. Did she miss the bright lights and fast living? Probably, he told himself glumly. How many obstacles would he have to knock down before he conquered the dragon and won the pretty girl? Something told him there were more than he had bargained for. But with his attorney's persistence and his love for her leading the way, he'd get there or know the reason why.

That evening the four of them stood on a narrow sidewalk in downtown Los Angeles. "Is this it?" April stared at the small, almost minuscule sign that proclaimed the name and location of the club. "You'd think they'd have banners or flags or something."

"In this business, less is more exclusive," Catherine said as she checked the marquee next door. It proclaimed women in all sorts of undress doing wonderfully exotic dances and gyrations never before seen by man. "Maybe we're going to the wrong place. Next door probably has more comedy and better acts," she inserted just before Sam took her arm and purposefully led her away to follow Jace through the small, nondescript door.

The entry was plain. Two large double doors led into the main room, but before entering everyone had to sign in and be given an okay by a man who looked as if he knew intimately Al Capone's mob years ago.

The inside was completely different. Decorated lavishly in shades of peach and navy blue, the large room was exquisite. The navy carpet was thick piled, the small tables a laminated white, while the chairs were peach and comfortably thick-cushioned. The stage was in the center, the bandstand up on one of the balconied walls.

"Do you have money in this, Jace?" Sam asked under his breath. "If so, I want in, too."

"Don't I wish," Jace whispered back. "But like the smart businessman I am, I turned the owner down. I thought he was too pushy for my tastes. He seemed to think 'Old Hollywood' was still in and that my life-style was a little too dull."

April patted his arm, a mischievous smile perking her lips. "Poor thing. It's tough being a sex symbol and Mr. Straight at the same time." She gave him an evil-eyed glance. "Just don't forget which is the real you."

Jace sighed. "I know. It could get me in a heap of trouble."

The conversation was light and fun, the drinks served in crystal glasses engraved with the club's initials. Sam leaned back and relaxed. After watching Catherine and Jace for over an hour he knew that she had spoken the truth concerning their relationship. He hoped.

An excellent new singer came on and did three numbers, her humor in between the songs just on the bawdy side. Then came a new and talented comedian discussing how hard it was to find an ugly girl in Los Angeles.

Sam let his eyes wander over to Catherine. She was looking very relaxed, more than he had seen her in a long time. Her eyes sparkled with warmth and fun, her manner was easygoing. Her walls were down and, to Sam, it was like a surprise birthday present. He reveled in it.

Suddenly a drum roll called for attention at center stage, just one table away, and spotlights began searching the room. Sam's stomach knotted, knowing intuitively that Catherine wouldn't like what was coming.

"Ladies and gentlemen, we have some celebrities in our midst tonight. I'm proud to introduce Jace Sullivan!"

Jace leaned over to Sam. "See what I mean? That guy will do anything for publicity." Then he stood and gave a short bow to the clapping audience.

The announcer droned on. "Jace Sullivan is up for an Academy Award for Best Actor in *Goodbye Spring*. Good luck, Jace!"

Jace smiled but beneath his breath he muttered to Sam, "You'd think this guy knew me!"

Catherine leaned forward, delight at the news showing on her face. "Congratulations, Jace! I didn't know."

His grin was sheepish as he sat down. "It won't be announced until tomorrow. April and I were going to tell you two later tonight."

"And sitting at his table is the beautiful and talented Catherine Sinclair!" the announcer proudly told the audience.

Sam could feel her muscles tighten, her smile become fixed. She stood on wobbly legs, blew a kiss and then sat down, only the spotlight didn't leave.

"Perhaps if we all clapped hard enough, we could get Kitty Sinclair to sing us just one song!" the man went on.

Catherine's face turned white as she shook her head back and forth. Her hand clenched Sam's like a vise. "Sam," she said in a strangled voice. "Please..."

With a deep-seated anger just barely under control, he rose and approached the announcer. The man with the big grin bent down in order to hear him, the expression on his face telling Sam that he knew Catherine wouldn't turn him down. Not in public.

"Miss Sinclair would be happy to sing for you. Now, if you'll just give me your name and address so I can mail you an invoice for her fee...."

His grin turned to a frown for just a moment, until he realized that the audience was watching. He grinned again, saying through his teeth. "What the hell are you talking about? This is good publicity for her! I'm only asking for one song!"

"So does everyone else," Sam said calmly, ignoring the panic in the other man's tone. The bastard deserved whatever he got by putting others on the spot. Let him wiggle out of this one on his own. "That's why we came up with this arrangement. Miss Sinclair doesn't sing unless she's paid, just like you don't serve drinks unless they're paid for. We'd all be out of business soon, if we didn't charge, wouldn't we?"

"What am I going to tell the audience?" the man hissed back.

"Tell them she has a sore throat and only came here tonight in order to be with you on this very important occasion," Sam said, suddenly angry enough to let it show. Did she find herself in this position often? Did people actually believe that singers could sing on the spot, no music, no preparation? Didn't they know singers' voices were their livelihood and had to be prepared? "Tell them anything you damn well want, but don't muddy her name or we'll see you in court."

Before the announcer could even begin his speech, Sam was back at the table and sitting next to Catherine, holding her hand to reassure her silently. Her expression was calm, but he could still feel the tenseness that seemed to emanate from her. She was scared to death.

His Catherine, a tiny mite that fought like a tiger, was frightened of singing in public. He wanted to enfold her in his arms, hold her close so that no one could hurt her.

It was as if there were two women inside Catherine Sinclair, he mused. One was the classy, sophisticated, shrewd lady he had met in his office and heard when she was conducting business with her agent. She was competent and sure of herself, cautious with even platonic relationships.

But the other Catherine Sinclair was here with him now. The other Catherine Sinclair was warm and funny and sometimes scared, like the time she maced the mouse and asked him to hold her tight in the middle of the night. Or like now, when she was frightened of performing. That same frightened lady would also smile sadly, her hugs turning into other things, such as lovemaking with an abandon and tenderness that few women possessed. Two women . . .

The announcer gave his apologies to the audience, then quickly went on to the next celebrity. Sam could feel Catherine go limp.

"That cuts it for me," Jace said, reaching for his wallet. "Let's get out of here before I punch someone in the nose for that cute trick. Besides, April's going to die from curiosity if she doesn't find out what you said to that snake to make him back off."

April and Catherine both stared at Jace in wonder. "How convenient to blame curiosity on others," April murmured, reaching for her fur wrap. "But you're right, we've got to get out of here before *I* punch him in the nose. Catherine can watch us both wiggle in curiosity all the way to a restaurant. I want coffee and something that tastes so sweet it's sickly."

They left quietly, Sam with his arm around Catherine, April with her eyes dancing as she watched them, and Jace dying of curiosity.

A diner on the outskirts of the city was their choice. It was really an old railroad car, but Sam promised the best pies in the state, and April couldn't wait to get in the door and try some.

Coffee was served immediately and Catherine sat back, enjoying the easy banter among the three friends. She felt a part of them now, included and enjoyed. Any comment she gave was listened to and treated as if her opinion was of value. A warm glow lit her stomach. This was what friendship was all about. How wrong she had been to confuse acquaintances with friends. Friendship was a rare gift not given to all, while acquaintances were a dime a dozen.

She glanced at Sam as he explained what had happened at the edge of the stage, not tensing, not even minding that he'd made public his role of protector. His brown hair fell slightly onto his forehead and an easy hand brushed it back. A grin made his eyes crinkle in the corners and parenthesized his mouth beguilingly. His jaw was strong, his chest working up and down as he slowly breathed. Pungent after-shave drifted toward her, enveloping her with feelings that were all mixed up. She felt loved, sexy and safe. She had to grin to herself on that one. What a combination! But it was true. With Sam, she felt all those things and because of it she felt one more thing: something she couldn't define but that squeezed her heart gently, like a hug.

"So I just told him he could see us in court," Sam finished, sipping his coffee.

"Wow," April whispered. "I'll have to remember that one. Jace never gets asked to act something, but he's always used for public appearances, such as tonight, and sometimes I think they'd like him better if he showed up with a film clip under his arm."

"Is that why you never go out much?" Catherine asked, watching April polish off her pie and then begin on Jace's under his watchful but humor-filled eyes.

"I'm afraid so. I love my fans, but I'm not too thrilled being the object of a promoter's desire," Jace said, his eyes widening in wonder as he watched April take the last bite of his dessert, then eye Sam's.

Sam grabbed his plate protectively. "No, you don't, April. This is mine, and I'm a growing boy who needs his energy."

"Then eat it and stop griping," April snapped, her desire for his pie turning into thwarted irritation.

Sam's eyes grew big while Jace began chuckling. His chuckles grew into full blown laughter. "Honey, I think the least you could do is tell your partner our secret. He'll think I'm starving you at home if you keep this up."

April's look was sheepish. "I'm sorry, Sam. I've just been craving something sweet today." She gave Jace a sideways glance that was supposed to silence him. It didn't work, so when he opened his mouth to speak she quickly beat him to it. "But what Jace is saying is that we're going to have miniatures of the big galoot next to me. He thinks it's wonderful, but this eating for all of us is killing me!"

"Really?" Catherine's eyes lit. "Jace, that's wonderful!" Her hand covered his across the table. "Congratulations!"

"Don't congratulate him!" April moaned. "He didn't do a darn thing except what came naturally. I'm the one who has the work ahead of me. He'll just sit around looking proud as a peacock and reap the reward of carbon copies!"

"Copies? How many are you planning to have?" Sam asked, his brows raised. "A legion?"

"Three," she said, awed herself. "The doctor says three and they'll be here in six months."

"Six months! You mean you've known for the past three months and never said a word?" Sam looked stunned, and both April and Catherine chuckled, although Catherine was a little amazed herself. Triplets!

"No, only for the past month. Officially, at least. I knew something was going awry when I couldn't button my suits or slip into my dresses."

4 BOOKS AND A SURPRISE GIFT

Here's a sweetheart of an offer that will put a smile on your lips...and 4 free Harlequin romances in your hands. Plus you'll get a secret gift, as well.

As a subscriber, you'll receive 4 new books to preview every month. Always before they're available in stores. Always for less than the retail price. Always with the right to return the shipment and owe nothing.

YES Please send me 4 **free** Harlequin Temptation novels and my **free** surprise gift. Then send me 4 new Harlequin Temptations each month. Bill me for only $1.99 each (for a total of $7.95 per shipment — a savings of $1.04 off the retail price) with no extra charges for shipping and handling. I can return a shipment and cancel anytime. The 4 free books and surprise gift are mine to keep!

142 C1X MDGA

NAME_____

ADDRESS_____APT._____

CITY_____

STATE_____ZIP CODE_____

Offer limited to one per household and not valid for present subscribers.
Prices subject to change.

AS A HARLEQUIN SUBSCRIBER, YOU'LL RECEIVE FREE...

- our monthly newsletter **Heart To Heart**
- our magazine **Romance Digest**
- special-edition **Harlequin Bestsellers** to preview for ten days without obligation

So kiss and tell us you'll give your heart to Harlequin.

"And I knew when her blouses were too, uh, tight, but she wouldn't listen to me," Jace inserted.

"You were too thrilled with the result to care whether I was pregnant or not," April teased.

Sam whistled. "So Brenda was right. I wonder how she knew?"

"Brenda?" all three chorused.

"Yes, Brenda. She said that April was into highs and lows lately."

"Wouldn't *you* be?" April shot back. "I keep thinking that if one is going to be chaos, think of what three will be. And I know nothing about raising children. Nothing!"

"Triplets." Catherine was in awe, as was Sam.

"My God," he muttered under his breath, a million questions popping into his mind but none voiced. "You're going to need that Academy Award just to be able to pay for diapers!"

Jace grinned with pride at their expressions, ignoring Sam's last comment. "April has an entire library of how-to-parent books, acquired at an astounding cost I might add. She'll be the best-read mother-to-be in the entire country."

"I don't have an entire library of books!"

"Two hundred, then," he corrected himself.

April looked mollified and Catherine couldn't help but laugh.

April leaned back, silently admitting with a sigh that Sam's pie couldn't be hers. She smiled brightly, ready to change the subject. "How's the case of the missing necklace coming? Any clues?"

"Not yet," Sam said guardedly, remembering the locksmith who had changed the locks yesterday. He hadn't told Catherine yet. He hadn't even told her about the private-eye firm he had hired. Later. Much later.

Jace frowned. "Have you made up a list of suspects, Catherine? It has to be someone you know who would write such horrible stuff."

Catherine nodded. "We did that when the police interviewed me. I don't know a soul who could be so vindictive." She ignored Sam's intensive look. She knew he was thinking of her mother, but there was no way. She had already checked, and her mother was still in the sanitarium.

"No black-sheep brother, father, relative who wants your money?"

Suddenly her face went blank. Her mouth worked, but no words came out. *No relative who wants your money?* Why hadn't she thought of that? The thief wasn't really after her, he wanted her money!

The table was still as they all waited for her to say something. But she couldn't speak. The words wouldn't form, her mind spun with the possibilities. Of course! Why hadn't she thought of it? Had she been so blind she couldn't see what was right in front of her eyes? Or had she just not wanted to see? Or was she just plain stupid, as some people believed? She couldn't answer her own questions because she didn't really know.

"Catherine?" Sam's warm hand closed over her cold one, pulling her back into the safety of the diner and out of her own, self-conceived nightmare. "What is it?"

She gave a nervous, high-pitched laugh. "Nothing. I think I'm still suffering from aftershock about April's triplets."

"Now you know what I'm going through," April said dryly, but her eyes showed she wasn't fooled a bit. "I don't know how I'll manage the house, Jace, work and three children all at the same time."

"You don't manage the house and Jace now, why would you then?" Jace teased, knowing that whatever had hit Catherine, she needed time to recuperate.

"I manage the maid and housekeeper who manage the house. And I do so, manage you. You're here tonight, aren't you? Who found your tie and your left shoe?"

"You found the tie because it was in *your* closet, where you put it after you wore it. I found the shoe under your robe."

"Well," she said compromising, "one out of two isn't bad."

ONE HOUR and another dessert later they had left the diner and called it a night. Jace and April dropped Sam and Catherine off, refused a nightcap and drove off into the evening.

The moment Sam touched the lock with his key, the lights came on to welcome them.

At Catherine's puzzled look, he explained. "A security device. You haven't seen it because it's on a timer that works only at night."

She nodded, somehow reassured. Even if Sam weren't there she'd feel safer. She almost asked him about the locks on her house, but didn't want to know the answer. With Sam she felt safe and needed. When she had to leave him to return to her home, she'd be alone. The thought of being by herself had never frightened her before, but now, she knew she'd miss Sam more than she ever dreamed possible. Her fear of being alone had nothing to do with the robbery, although it troubled her. Her fear was that there would be an empty space in her life. A very big empty space. One that she just didn't want to think about for fear of having to put a label on it—a label like love.

They stood in the hallway, Sam turning her around in his arms. His hands traveled from her elbows to her slim shoulders as if warming her. "Tired?" he murmured softly, and she nodded her head.

"What did you think of in the restaurant, Catherine?" He hated to ask her now, when the violet shadows under her eyes confirmed her state of mind and physical condition, but he had to know.

"Nothing." She stared up at him, one hand reaching up to rest against the firmness of his jaw as if to reassure herself that he was really there. She could feel his pulse beating. "Sam? Please hold me. Hold me close," she whispered.

He enfolded her in his arms, resting his head on top of hers. "All night long, darling," he said quietly. "All night long." He could get his answers in the morning when she was rested. Right now, all he wanted to do was to hold her, too.

And he did.

10

THE PRIVATE INVESTIGATOR called late Friday morning. Sam was sitting at the desk in his study, putting signatures to the letters that Brenda had brought over earlier. He could hear Catherine humming in the kitchen as she kneaded dough for a new pastry she had wanted to try. It was costing him a fortune in flour, but she could try anything she wanted as long as it was in his home, in his kitchen. Hell, he'd buy her a flour mill if she wanted it.

"What have you found out?" Sam asked.

"Well," the man at the other end drawled. "The lady has plenty of enemies, but no one in particular. She's had a pretty tough life."

"I'm aware of that," Sam said impatiently. He didn't know much, but he could read between the lines of what Catherine had told him. Right now he was concerned with protecting her. Besides, to hear Catherine's life story from someone else almost seemed a betrayal. He wanted to know the facts, but he wanted her to tell him, not some stranger. "What else?"

"It wasn't her mother. We checked on that. It wasn't her father, 'cause he's been working on the docks in New York for the past twenty-two years. He's had no more than a day off in the past three months. Besides, he won't even acknowledge her. She doesn't have any agents or promoters angry with her and no one in Nashville or Dallas seems to have a bone to pick." The man hesitated, as if waiting for an answer to drop in his lap.

"And?"

"And nothing. That's it so far. There was a man in the vicinity of her home, an older man, shabbily dressed. He was seen walking along the road on two occasions. But no one's seen him since. He could have been one of the new or temporary gardeners around the neighborhood. No one seems to do their own lawns around here." The detective said it as if he thought everyone should.

"Are the locks changed?"

"Yes. I have the keys. All of them."

"Good. Now, find something, anything, that gives us a clue."

"Have you asked the little lady?" the man returned dryly. "Seems to me that it has to be someone she knows."

"Good thinking." Sam's voice was equally dry. "And the police have already been that route. Why do you think I hired you?"

"Okay, okay," the other man said tiredly. "I've got three men working around the clock. But if you find out anything unusual, let us know. We need something, some handle to put on this before we can get any closer to solving the riddle. Right now, I haven't got a thing and house-sitting isn't doing us any good."

"I know. Thanks," Sam said before placing the phone back in its cradle. His stomach was taut with tension. Catherine. Catherine. Catherine. His mind played her name over and over again like an old tune. He loved her. He loved her so much it hurt, yet he couldn't seem to protect her. He couldn't protect her because she wouldn't protect herself by helping him. Frustration reached out to enfold him. He couldn't get Catherine until he caught the robber.

Easy, Sam, old boy, he told himself. *Patience is a virtue—probably the only one you have. So use it.*

CATHERINE'S STRUDEL turned out like a picture from a magazine, which was where she had gotten the recipe. Filled with nuts and raisins and coated with cinnamon and a light glaze, it was enough to make a mouth water. She was proud of it and of herself. She quickly made coffee and set out a tray. Sam would enjoy a piece of this. She grinned. So would April if she were here. April would probably eat the whole thing. Maybe she'd have Brenda take her a piece.

As she worked she hummed an old song that had won her her first gold record. Funny how music came so quickly to mind when she was in Sam's kitchen. As soon as she thought about performing again, though, the music fled as if it were nothing but wisps of gray smoke. And it left nothing behind, no lyrics, no snatches of bridges. Only a tight lump in her throat. She had felt this way ever since her last concert. The doctors had told her it was exhaustion. . . .

But today she wouldn't let the thought bother her. Today Sam was home and she felt safe. Happy. Loved. She knew, without him saying it, that he loved her deeply. It didn't matter that she didn't want him to. What mattered was he had found something in her to love. He reaffirmed her belief in herself that she wasn't a wicked woman, something to sneer or laugh at. She wasn't something to brush off the bottoms of boots. Sam was an honest, clear-thinking man and he knew the value of people. In his heart he had given her value, deserved or not.

After placing two cloth napkins in their rings, she picked up the tray and walked toward Sam's study. She heard the curtness of his voice, then the clink of the phone as it was placed back in the cradle. Business? She hoped not. Whether he knew it or not, he was as much in need of a vacation as she was.

"Sam? Care for some company?" she said brightly as she pushed open the door to see him sitting at his desk, the tight lines around his mouth proclaiming his agitation. But the moment he saw her, out came his boyish, heart-stopping smile to warm up her thoughts.

"I'd love some."

She smiled away the uneasiness. "Good, move those letters so I can put this darn thing down."

He snapped to, doing as he was told as if she were a general. She couldn't help the smile that graced her lips. Sam only did what *he* wanted to, unless it was in his best interests to do otherwise. He waited until she eased the tray in front of him, then circled her waist with his hands, pulling her down on his lap.

"Let's sit here and talk and see what comes up," he said, leering at her playfully.

Her brows drew together in a scowl although she could hardly keep her smile at bay. "Sam Lewis, that's the oldest and one of the crudest lines in history. Surely you're more original than that!"

"Lady, if you call that crude, you should have been in the military with me. They came up with lines that would have stripped the polish off your toenails."

She grinned, unable to keep a straight face. Her arms

circled his neck as she tipped her head to one side. "Oh, yeah? Tell me some," she said in a throaty voice. She felt light and fun and sexy and happy, and it was all Sam's doing.

He whispered a couple of off-color lines in her ear, and she blushed. He chuckled, a deep hearty sound that reverberated in his large chest, and she responded to his chuckle with a giggle of her own.

Her eyes focused on his and slowly, very slowly, her smile disappeared. Their laughter was replaced by a tension that flowed between them like a current, gaining strength with every passing second. It was almost visible, pulling them together against their will, as if they had no choice in what they were doing.

His kiss was dark with need and brilliantly lit with love, and she responded in the same way. Her hands threaded through his hair, her lips seeking succor from his. Their breath mingled and was dispelled from their lungs as if it was too heady. They kissed deeply, each filling the need to touch the other's soul. Catherine felt herself slipping into another world where only Sam lived and where his hurts and thoughts and feelings were hers. They blended together in time until she didn't know whose hand was whose and where her lips began and his left off.

Finally he pulled away, his hand making sure that her head was resting on his shoulder. "Oh, Catherine," he said with a sigh. "What am I going to do? I can't seem to concentrate when you're around and I can't concentrate when you aren't around."

She kissed the side of his throat just above the pulse point. "Are you saying you can't concentrate, period, and want to blame something or someone, so you've decided to blame me?" Her tongue darted out to touch the very spot she kissed.

"Yes." His arms tightened around her waist and back, settling her more firmly against him. He wanted to feel her every muscle, every silken part of her.

"But why blame me? Why not blame yourself?" Her lips reached up to touch the underside of his jaw.

"Because it's hard to take the blame for the way I feel, since I've never felt this way before." He was being honest. He just wished she'd be the same. But instead of admitting her feelings, she kissed his jaw again. Exquisite agony was building up inside him, but he didn't stop her. Somewhere inside him was a need to be a masochist. He hadn't known he carried that need.

Her tongue reached out to tease him behind his ear. "Don't I get blamed for everything? Why should I take this, too?"

"What else do you take the blame for?" His voice was deep and gravelly. His temperature was rising and he knew it, but he was powerless to stop her. It felt too good, too right.

"Oh," she murmured before touching the outer shell of his ear. "Just about everything since I was three. I was the fault of the weather, the boss, the house, the men in my mother's life." Suddenly her foray stopped and she realized what secrets she had given away. The look on her face was one of amazement. Obviously she had never allowed her past to slip out accidentally before.

"And did you accept that awesome responsibility at the age of three? Or did you wait until later before you accepted it?" Sam's voice was light, but he silently prayed that she would answer him. He needed to know more about her. He loved her and wanted to know her inside out.

She hesitated only a moment before slowly answering, as if giving it all her consideration. "No, not at the age of three. I accepted it around the age of ten."

"How?"

"By trying to keep the bad weather out, praying for more money. Be keeping our small apartment as clean as I could. By staying out of the way."

"Did it work?"

Catherine smiled sadly. "No. There was always something else to be blamed for. So I found another route out. I used to take the bus into the wealthy sections of New Orleans. Then I'd sit on a bench and watch the rich kids at play. I mimicked them until I had their accents, knew their manners and could even dress like them, compliments of Goodwill."

He had to clear his throat before he could talk. "Chalk it all up to learning your craft at a young age." His arms tightened even more, as if he would never let her go.

"Oh, now it sounds a little soap operaish, but at the time it was the best teacher I could have had for getting along in the world. I learned my manners and how to win, bar nothing, from those rich people. They were more cutthroat in ways that the wharf kids could never have been. The rich ones did it with style, the poor were clumsy at knifing someone in the back."

"But you survived. That's something to be proud of. You survived and made something wonderful out of your own raw materials. You did it. With no one's help."

Catherine nodded her head, not trusting her voice. Sam was right. No matter what, she had escaped. That was something to be proud of. A frown marred her forehead. But now what? Where did she go from here? What would she do if the movie career didn't pan out? Make more records? Tour more cities? Work harder than she had? It all seemed so hopeless.

"When do I get the brass ring for all my efforts?" she wondered aloud.

"Now, baby. Right now." Sam stood, still holding her in his arms as he walked out of his study and toward the bedroom. "You deserve more than you've got only you don't know it. Let me give you back a little."

They made love with the blinds wide open and the sunlight streaming in. Her body was a glistening golden rainbow and he tenderly devoured each inch as though it were the last.

She writhed beneath him, wanting to share her feelings of joy but he wouldn't let her. He held her hands away from him, teasing her with lips and tongue. This was her time, her moment to enjoy, and because she enjoyed, then so would he.

With thoughts wrapped carefully in cotton batting and arms and limbs entwined, they slept. Coffee and cake could come later. They had just had the best dessert of all. . . each other.

THE WEEK HAD BEEN the most unsatisfyingly satisfying week Sam had ever had. Catherine was within his grasp, within his heart and mind. She had become more necessary to him every day, yet he felt as if she were wary, drifting away from him on purpose sometimes. He couldn't put his finger on the reasons involved but he knew that she had told him more than she had ever told anyone about her past. At first she had seemed comforted by his response, then she had become aggravated. He didn't know what to do.

By the time Sunday rolled around, he was so used to walking in and finding her there, he couldn't conceive of her *not* being a part of his life and home. But he knew that time was coming. He knew, and it felt like a cold piece of lead in his stomach. She would leave him. It was only a matter of time.

Monday morning left Sam with a feeling of reluctance to work at all, let alone go to the office and leave Catherine by herself all day. But there was no choice. Against his own logic, fear of Catherine leaving him began to grow by the hour. Then, when he returned home to find her there, he couldn't believe he had been so frightened. Until the next morning, when the cycle began again.

Tuesday was no better.

Neither was Wednesday.

By day he would worry, but at night he would wonder how he could be so apprehensive about the sweet woman in his arms. She must feel something for him. Something fairly strong or she wouldn't be so pleased to see him when he walked in the door every evening.

When he hit the office Thursday morning, he was chomping at the bit for the weekend to come. Then he wouldn't have to leave her for two whole days.

"Work is a pain in the neck," he muttered to Brenda as she gave him the day's mail.

"It may be, but I'll be darned if I've found a solution to lack of money that works as well as this." She grinned, an impish grin that lit her brown eyes with mischief. She was a very attractive woman in her own right, but she purposely played it down. He often wondered why, but he'd never asked.

Laying aside the letter in his hands, he stared up at her. "Brenda, why don't you let your hair down, instead of keeping it in that tight little bun? You're very attractive, but you try so hard not to show it."

"Oh, Lord, you noticed!" She gave a mock groan. "And after all my efforts to keep you at bay! Does this mean you're going to start chasing me around the desk every morning?"

He couldn't help teasing. "Do you want me to?"

"Well," she considered, tapping a nail against her cheek. "At least I'd get some daily exercise. As long as you promise not to catch me, that is."

"And if I did?"

"Then I'd have to hit you where it will hurt the most." It was a flat statement, no teasing involved.

Sam leaned back. "I'm crushed."

"Don't be. Even Burt Reynolds doesn't stand a chance with me. I've had enough of men to last me a lifetime, and certainly don't need any more guilt on my conscience."

"Is it that you don't like us as a group, or individually?" Now he was intrigued. Catherine was much the same way. What had made them take this path? How could he help Catherine? Perhaps if he understood Brenda, he would learn something about Catherine.

"Neither." She shrugged. "What is this? The Inquisition?"

"Curiosity."

Brenda peered at him intently. "Still holding your heart for Catherine Sinclair?" she asked.

He didn't answer. He nodded solemnly.

"Then let me tell you. The Catherine Sinclairs of this world are lucky. They have talent, beauty, money and men. And the men gravitate to them like seeds to watermelon. And sometimes, in their push to get to the best and the finest, they step on others. Usually other women—the ones in their way either by marriage or relationship. So, when a woman grows up and stops believing in fairy tales and handsome princes, she relies on herself and remembers that men don't beat paths to her door unless she's got something they can have immediately." She stared out the window a minute before continuing. "So I've decided that I'll never be used as a way station for some other woman's passenger. It's easier this way."

"My God," Sam muttered, staring in awe at Brenda. She had the same belief concerning Catherine that the press did. She thought she was "the girl who had everything," and Brenda couldn't see past another woman's facade because she was so busy building her own. Women were supposed to be a mystery to men, but obviously they were even a mystery to other women. It boggled his mind.

Brenda gave a nervous laugh as if to dispel the things she had just said. Sam could tell she was wishing that she had kept their conversation light and not given in to the impulse to bare her soul. "Well, maybe next time you won't ask." She smoothed the wrinkles from her black pin-striped skirt. "Maybe next time I won't talk so much."

"Brenda? What if I told you that you were wrong about Catherine?"

She smiled sadly. "Then I wouldn't say anything, but I would think that you're more naive than I am."

Sam sighed. "Okay, you win. Get Leo Coulter on the phone for me, would you? I'm supposed to make an appointment for lunch with him. Something about a divorce case that has all the makings of a huge trial."

"Are you sure he's a working attorney? Every time you two try to get together, he's got some kind of female getting in the way."

"He's one of the hardest working attorneys I know. But yes, he does like female company. It's probably because he's never been able to date much before. He was so poor he made me look like Rockefeller."

"Humph," Brenda said disbelievingly as she walked out the office door.

Sam grinned. What he really ought to do was get Brenda and Leo together. That would teach both of them a thing or two. Leo didn't believe that there was a woman who couldn't be bought with prestige or money, and Brenda . . . well, Sam now knew how Brenda felt.

He heard the phone buzz, then Brenda's head popped around the door. "Phone. The private investigator you hired."

His action was quick. He picked up the phone and barked a hello into it, anxious to hear what had been discovered.

"Mr. Lewis. It's her father."

A light film of sweat glistened on his forehead. "I thought you told me he was working in New York."

"Sorry. I meant her stepfather. He hitched up here from New Orleans. I think he means to see her again."

"Where is he now?"

"He's here at the house, but we've got to let him go

unless you want to call the police and press charges. He's staying at a small motel off one of the main highways. He says he already pawned the stereo and TV, and all he has left is the necklace, and that it's in a safe place."

"Drive him back to the motel. Tell him his daughter's with me and to call me in the morning and we'll arrange a meeting." His voice was like hard concrete. "Tell him that I'll deal with him tomorrow."

"Right. By the way, he got her address from her agent. He pretended to be a male nurse from her mother's sanitarium."

"I'll take care of that."

Sam's hand was shaking by the time he hung up the phone. Could Catherine's stepfather hate her so much he would steal from her and—to top it all off—frighten her to death with stupid, crude messages left on every mirror? My God! What kind of animals raised her?

Suddenly he wanted to drag Brenda in here and tell her Catherine's story. He wanted Brenda to realize just how much a woman with beauty, brains, talent and money suffered . . . and at the hands of a man who hated her so much he would try to mess with her own shaky image of herself.

But Sam couldn't.

COMING HOME had become a ritual to Sam. Just slipping the key in the lock and opening the door to a host of delicious smells, anything from perfume to dessert, was a treat in itself. But the best treat was Catherine's greeting.

"Hi," she said, a big happy smile on her face as she walked down the hall toward him.

And he always said and did the same thing. "Hi," he murmured, opening his arms and waiting for her to step into them before they closed like a net around her. He breathed in the fragrance of her hair, the soap she used. He felt the small-boned skeleton of her and treasured her all the more for it.

But tonight, he had news, only it would wait. He wasn't about to spoil his homecoming by giving her details of her very nasty relatives. He'd do it later. Perhaps even tomorrow.

Catherine reached on tiptoe to give a second kiss to the tip of his nose. "Hungry?"

"Starved." He grinned. "What do you have in mind?"

"Birds' feathers and horsehair in sand gravy." Trying to repress her smile was like trying to repress the sun. It peeped out and then brightened his whole being.

His arms rested around her slim waist, his fingers hooked together. "If you cooked it, I'll eat it."

Her perfectly etched brows rose. "Confident in my ability?"

"No, I just wouldn't notice what I was eating if you're across the table from me," he answered honestly, then saw the wariness flick in her eyes before she shooed it away.

"Tsk, tsk, tsk. You're too trusting. That's dangerous."

"Only with you, my dear." He played the part of the bad wolf, but she didn't buy it.

"How do you know I wouldn't harm you, Sam?" Her face was sad, yet earnest. It was almost as if she was afraid of hurting him, but knew it was inevitable.

"I don't. But it's my chance to take."

Then his lips claimed hers, and he shut out all troubled thoughts from her mind. And his.

DINNER WAS DELICIOUS. Dessert was baked apples with cinnamon and cream. It was one of those desserts Sam had always read about, but had never eaten. No one had ever taken the time to fix them for him before. Already in love with Catherine, he was now head over heels in love with her cooking. If he could keep her with him, he saw the future as one large feast after another... along with many more pounds than his body carried now.

After dinner they watched a made-for-TV movie that didn't quite follow the plot of the book they had both just read. They giggled their way through the dopey commercials. They ate popcorn and he drank white wine, the perfect combination as far as Sam was concerned.

"No class," Catherine had mumbled around her popcorn when he had offered it to her.

He leaned back to rest against the sofa, his legs stretched out on the floor in front of him so she could snuggle between them, toboggan style. He kissed the nape of her neck. "I know. Isn't it wonderful?"

"Wonderful," she said, bending her head back to be more accommodating to his lips.

"A bowl of popcorn, wine and thou. How happy can a guy get?"

"And a movie that you already know the plot to."

"Nope. I thought we agreed." He kissed between sentences. "This isn't the right movie. Somebody just bought the title and character's names and made up a whole new story."

Catherine twisted her neck. "You missed a spot."

"Where?" His lips grazed the entire back of her neck,

only stopping to kiss the softness just under her right ear.

She sighed. "That was it."

"I knew I'd find it sooner or later."

Catherine leaned back in Sam's arms and gave a small sigh of contentment. Was it possible to feel this happy, this right with another person? She never would have believed it. But Sam was becoming everything to her, and with him she didn't need anything else. The thought was comforting instead of terrifying, but she didn't stop to analyze it. She just reveled in it.

In the back of her mind was still her home up in the canyons, but since Sam hadn't brought up the fact that the locks had been changed, neither had she. The police had requested it and Sam had said he would take care of it, but no word had been uttered since. They were both floating along on a raft down a quiet river of peace, and neither wanted to head for shore yet. It was too special, too wonderful, just to be where they were.

Until the doorbell rang. Sam groaned and Catherine moaned.

"It better be good, it's almost midnight," he said, standing and tucking his shirt into the waistband of his pants.

But when the door opened, Sam knew that everything had changed. An old man stood on the porch. In worn baggy tan trousers, a faded denim shirt that still held the leftovers of yesterday's breakfast and a fedora on his head, he looked as if he could have been transplanted anywhere, and he still would have been a has-been. In his hand was a small flight bag.

His smile was lethal, and with a sinking feeling deep in the pit of his stomach, Sam knew who he was.

"Mr. Samuel Lewis?"

"Yes," he braved, hoping against hope he was wrong. If Catherine had been raised by this, this . . .

"I'm Kitty Slovak's papa, Grady Turner. Most folks call me Grady." The older man held out his hand as if this were a cocktail party. Sam stared at it.

"Sam," Catherine began as she walked toward the front door only to stop in midstep. Her hand clenched at her stomach. "No," she finally whispered, and a bleakness came to her eyes that Sam hadn't seen since that first day in his office.

"I need to talk to ya', sweetheart," Grady said, looking meaningfully at Catherine.

"No, you don't. You need to talk to me," Sam said quietly but threads of steel laced his voice.

Catherine stood still, her hand still clenching her stomach, her bright-blue eyes shadowed with doubts and fears Sam would probably never know the complete source of.

He ushered the man in and they sat down on the couch. "I believe you have something of Catherine's that you need to give back," Sam began.

"Kitty promised me money," he whined. "All I did was take it for collateral."

"Where is the necklace now?"

The man patted his flight bag. "Right here. Don't ya know, nobody wanted to lend me money on it. They thought I stole it."

"Which you did." Sam's voice would have told most people not to tread too closely to him, but this man must not have sensed the value in leaving well enough alone. "Just like you stole the TV and stereo."

"No, I jest borrowed them. Ask Catherine! She

wouldn't want her papa to be called a liar! Neither would her poor mama!" His rheumy eyes sought to beg from Catherine but she was curled up in the corner of the couch, watching him with eyes that didn't see. Her hands were trembling just as much as the old man's, only for different reasons.

"Hand the necklace over."

"But the money..." the old man croaked before he finally recognized the threat in Sam's voice. Another glance at Catherine was enough to confirm the fact that she wouldn't help him.

"Hand it over or the cops will be here in less than five minutes. I'll have you under arrest and press charges you never dreamed of." The look in Sam's eyes was enough to convince Grady.

It took him several minutes before the zipper could be undone and the necklace rooted out, but it was finally accomplished. The old man grinned, one shaky hand holding up his trophy. "Here, here it is."

"Give it to me." Sam held out his hand and the necklace was plopped into it. His fingers clenched as if they were squeezing a neck.

"Now," Sam went on conversationally, "I'm calling a cab, paying for it in advance. It will take you to the Los Angeles Airport. You will have your ticket paid—one way—to New Orleans. You will never bother Catherine again, under any circumstances. Do you understand?"

"Now wait jest a cotton-pickin' minute. Let Catherine talk. She'll tell you that she's supposed to be takin' care of her mama and me. I don't have to listen to you. You're not my daughter!"

"And she's not your daughter, either," Sam growled, his anger showing clearly. "So you listen. Get out of here and out of her life or you'll be in jail. The police don't regard stealing as borrowing. Neither do they take kindly to destroying someone else's property. They'll be more than happy to put you where I'd like to."

The old man turned toward Catherine, his arms outstretched, his voice a whine. "Kitty, honey, tell this man that you gotta take care of us. Tell him, honey."

Sam stood, taking in a deep breath. His body was larger than it had ever looked, and Catherine's eyes darted to him, suddenly afraid.

"You get the hell out of here and never come back, or I'll put you in jail and keep you there so long you'll never see daylight again! After all the things you wrote on those mirrors, you don't deserve a thing! And I haven't even mentioned breaking and entering and theft." His voice was a growl from deep in his throat.

The old man seemed to know he had lost, but a sly smile came over his lips, showing teeth that were cracked and stained. "You'd have a hard time proving breaking and entering. I got the key and walked in the front door."

"Who gave you the key?" Sam wanted so badly to look at Catherine, but he was afraid to. He was scared of what he'd see.

"It was on a ledge above the screen door in the back. Most folks put an extra key out back somewhere. I jest had to look." He grinned again. "So you can drop those charges, Mr. Attorney," he said.

"You don't know the law very well or you'd know that the charges still stand. You were not an invited guest, therefore it was breaking and entering." Sam motioned toward the door. "You can wait at the curb for the taxi, but you're leaving now. Another attorney will

pick you up in New Orleans and describe the rest of the
arrangements to you."

"But, but—"

"No buts! Just get out of here before I break your
neck!"

SAM HUNG UP the telephone and began stroking Catherine's back. She'd hardly said a word since her stepfather walked in the door. Almost like a robot, she had followed Sam into his study, then sat across from him while he made several calls. But he couldn't stand the distance between them. He had finally gone over and picked her up, holding her close to him as he warmed her body with his own. She was curled up in his lap now, listening while he made the rest of the necessary phone calls that would get that damn family of hers out of her life, for good.

Grady would be picked up by another attorney and taken back to the apartment he'd shared with Catherine's mother. There would be food in the house, but no money would ever be given to him. Apartment and utility bills would be paid, clothing would be bought, but it would all be done with the aid of a counselor there. If, just once, that man tried to reach or speak to Catherine again, all monies would stop instantly. There would be no second chance.

"Are you all right?" he asked quietly, and Catherine nodded her head, afraid to look into his eyes to see the hate and derision there.

He had found the culprit, and she wasn't sure she was pleased or more frightened than ever. Why couldn't things have just gone on forever just as they were? Why did Sam have to find out just how despicable she, her family and roots were? In the space of minutes her magic dream world with Sam had crumpled, just like a house made of cards. God, it hurt!

She told herself that it was bound to have happened sooner or later because she hadn't confronted the situation head on, and when that happened, the situation had a way of confronting you. She should have handled it sooner. She should have done something, taken some action, not let things drift along until events snowballed and there was no time to act.

With a flick of his wrist, Sam turned out his desk lamp and stood, carrying Catherine in his arms as he walked out of the darkened room and toward the bedroom.

"I can walk, Sam. Let me down." Her voice was low and deep and hurting but she couldn't hide her feelings tonight. Tomorrow...but not tonight.

"Just relax. I want to carry you." His voice was soft, but firm all the same. His chest and shoulders moved with each step and she could feel the flexing muscles beneath. Somehow that comforted her and made her sad at the same time. How wonderful it would have been to stay like this, with Sam, forever. How so very wonderful....

He didn't put her down until he reached the bed, then placed her gently in the center. As if they were in no hurry, they undressed for bed, neither being coy or sexy.

Catherine finished first and climbed between the sheets. She watched Sam, not with the eyes of a lover but with the eyes of someone in love. He was beautiful.

Strong arms and chest that tapered down to slim hips and firm thighs. But his eyes were the best feature of all. His face showed the strength of character and the humor he found in life, but his eyes showed the tenderness that he was so capable of. Some might look at him and think he was too soft, but Catherine knew better. He was rock hard when it came to getting what he wanted. He was firm and yet never a bully. And she loved him with all her heart.

The notion of her loving him was also firm and strong, without the feeling of surprise that she thought she should have felt. Her love for him washed over her like warm water gently lapping at a shore. It was right and peaceful and inevitable.

He slipped between the sheets and his arms enclosed her. She rested her head against his chest and closed her eyes, giving a small sigh of contentment. She would enjoy this closeness with him now. It would have to last for a long time. Her hand rested on the flat plane of his stomach, her touch reassuring her that he was real. She was asleep almost immediately.

Sam stared at the ceiling, a small smile tugging at the corners of his mouth. If he had been a teenager right now, he might have jumped up and down and whooped up a storm, then run to the nearest tree to carve a big heart that said "Sam loves Catherine."

But he was an adult and all he could do was smile crazily at the ceiling, tighten his hold on the one person he loved and think of the future.

The mystery was solved and her stepfather gone. Now he could concentrate on Catherine and hopefully make her fall in love with him.

But what about your lack of money, his conscience asked. I'll make more, he silently answered. Besides, she wasn't poor. They could split the bills and both still have enough leftover. And he would always pay when they dined out. *What about her career?* She can do anything she pleases. I'll just be there for her when she needs me, he answered again, but the niggling truth was that he wanted her here with him, not on the road doing one-night stands across the country. He wanted her in his arms at night, in his home when he arrived. *Male chauvinist!* I know, I know. I said that's what I wanted, not what I would settle for. I'll settle for anything that keeps Catherine by my side. He closed his eyes and rested his cheek against the top of her head, taking a deep breath of the perfume of her hair. When he drifted into sleep, the smile on his face was still there.

CATHERINE WOKE just before dawn. Her head was still on Sam's chest. She moved slowly, cautiously, afraid to wake him yet knowing his arm must be pins and needles.

A lock of brown hair had fallen over his forehead, a small tinge of a smile graced his lips, making the crinkles at the corner of his eyes more noticeable. He was so handsome, so beautiful, so perfect. Well, maybe not perfect, just perfect looking, she conceded wryly, remembering some of their arguments.

Then the smile left her face. She had to leave today. She had to find peace with herself before she could ever find peace with someone else. She had to leave him before she spewed on him the venom life had built up in her. When he finally put two and two together, he would hate her for her past. It would never work between them. Never.

He groaned, then began snoring softly, and a need so perfect and so primitive washed over her. Before she could even control it, her hand reached out to stroke his chest and feel the furring there. Her hand rose and fell with his even breathing, making her even more aware of the life force that filled him. She wanted him.

His eyes opened to slits and stared back at her, almost immediately telegraphing the same needs and adding fuel to her already-out-of-control fire. His hand reached out to touch her breast, cup it. Her hand followed the same pattern on his chest and they teased each other with promises of fulfillment. Shallow breathing was the only sound in the room.

Sam rolled toward her, finally unable to contain his caresses to just one part of her. He wanted all of her, wanted every inch of her velvet smooth skin pressed against him until he dissolved inside her so they could never be separated again.

Tears like dewdrops graced Catherine's cheeks as she smiled at him, her hand stroking his jaw as if to burn the memory of him into the palm of her hand. He kissed the tears away, then lingered to taste the sweetness of her mouth as it opened to invite him in.

His hands traveled her abdomen and thighs, caressing the skin with his fingertips, making love to her in Braille so that she would know that not only his words showed the depth of his feelings, but his whole body also. He knew she understood. He loved her.

His lips followed the same path as his hands, reaching tender areas that brought a blush to Catherine's milky skin. He chuckled softly in the dimness. "Don't move away, Catherine. I promise I won't hurt you," he murmured.

Still she pulled away, drawing his shoulders back up to her level. "Please, Sam," she said throatily, still blushing. "I need you now."

He chuckled again, giving her a light squeeze. "It's nice to be so needed," he teased. "And I can't disappoint my Lady Love."

Bending down he took one rosy tip in his mouth and sucked gently. From far away, he heard her small groan of pleasure and doubled his efforts.

His strong lean body finally came to rest on top of hers and they synchronized as never before. With each thrust he felt her answer as they rode toward a spiral of heat and color and a complete sense of oneness.

Then slowly, ever so slowly, he kissed her neck and cheeks, telling her silently again just how much she meant to him. Soon he slept with her curled against his body. One hand rested possessively on her breast, as if to reassure himself of her presence.

Sometime early in the morning, Sam stirred. He turned to reach for Catherine, finding only a cold pillow in her place. He raised his head, glancing about the room. None of her clothing was strewn around. Everything was in order. He listened for sounds from other parts of the house. There were none.

His skin prickled with dread.

He called her name. "Catherine?"

Nothing.

He called again. "Catherine?"

Nothing.

Without knowing how, he knew that she was gone, but he had to prove it to himself.

He slipped from the bed and threw on his slacks,

hitching the snap and zipper as he walked down the hall toward the kitchen. It was empty.

He checked each room, his heart thudding harder and heavier with every step.

His fears were confirmed when he reached the study. On his desk, next to the phone were the Yellow Pages. They were opened to the taxi companies. Next to the book was a scribbled note, written in obvious haste.

Sam,
Thanks for all your help, but it's time I helped myself now. Please, let's leave this relationship where it is and not see each other again. That way we can both have our memories.

Kitty Slovak

His fist came down with a bang. "Damn, Catherine! Why?"

He slumped in his desk chair and stared at the note, willing it to disappear, imagining he could hear Catherine's voice coming from the kitchen. Suddenly the pain in his chest was so strong he could hardly breathe. She wasn't coming back. She hadn't made a trip to the store and would return soon. She was gone.

For the first time since he was twelve and had wrecked his bike, he cried. Great gulping sobs that made his throat ache and blinded him with salty tears.

"TOMMY? CATHERINE, HERE. Get a messenger service to send the sheet music over to the Beverly Hills Hotel so I can begin studying it." Catherine sat in the plush bungalow, twisting the cord of the phone as she tried to block out all thoughts except one—get back to work.

"Right, honey," the agent said, a smile in his voice. "But what are you doing at the hotel? I thought you were staying with that attorney fella?"

"I was. Now I'm not. And, Tommy, don't let anyone, *anyone* know where I am."

"Right, honey. But you know you have a few questions to answer when I see you."

She scraped back her hair from the side of her face, her hands shaking. "Right," she muttered before hanging up.

Putting both the pillows behind her, she leaned back in the bed and closed her eyes to keep the tears at bay.

Sam, her heart cried and her mind responded. She was running again. Only this time she was running away from love, the one thing she had sworn that when she found it she would never let it go. She held her head with shaking hands, willing the ache to go away.

But she had no choice. Her heart had almost broken when she had quietly packed her bags and called the cab this morning. Against her better judgment, she had tiptoed in to see Sam once more, fighting the desire to kiss his forehead. He had been in a deep sleep, his arm still stretched out as if she was there. She couldn't make up her mind then whether to laugh or cry. He looked like the perfect choice for a hero until his cheeks dimpled from a funny thought or dream—then he looked like a little boy about to do some delightful mischief. It was almost her undoing.

But she steeled herself to leave, knowing that to stay would eventually kill his love. How could he still love her, really love her and not feel pity, when he knew all about her background?

And she needed time to think. Time to sort out the

mess she had made of her life and see if she could pull herself back together. Sam would help, she knew, but then she might never learn what was really important to her and where her priorities should lie.

This way was better. Better for him. Although she didn't know if she could really believe that this hurt would make her a better person. She sniffed. Character-building? She almost choked on that one. She'd had enough happen to her in the past to build enough character for ten!

Not like Sam, though. He had built his own character, and it was firm where she was brittle, his was soft where she had none, his was tender when she didn't know what it was like. He was so vulnerable, and she was afraid of hurting him more by staying than by leaving. He was so good. So very, very good. And he made her feel that way, too. While she had been with him she had felt good and honest and wanted and needed...and happier than she had ever been before.

So why did she leave? She couldn't answer the question entirely. She was all mixed up and she couldn't seem to put her thoughts into any proper order. All she knew was that she would contaminate him by asking for his help with the problems she had created.

She knew she deeply loved Sam. And Sam wasn't the type to love forever—his past history had proven that. He would want to have a good stable relationship for a while, then move on to another girl, another toothbrush and another answering service. Oh, she knew about the phone calls that came in for Sam. He must have had an entire stable of girls after him constantly if his phone calls were anything to go by!

And that was not the kind of man who could change into a husband overnight.

The toothbrushes. In her quick flight this morning, she had still taken time to round up those damn toothbrushes and dump them all in the kitchen garbage can. She could have flogged herself for doing that! Would he see them and realize that even though she was leaving, she couldn't stand the thought of someone else taking her place? Would he know that although she couldn't have him, she cared so much that she couldn't allow someone else to have him, either? She prayed he wouldn't see the evidence of her folly.

Finally her thoughts and dreams stopped scurrying around like mice in the dark, and she slept. But her last thought was that she wished Sam were there to hold her close and tell her everything would be all right.

12

SAM UNLOCKED THE DOOR to his house and walked in, his feet dragging as he made his way to the kitchen and a quick shot of tequila. He should drink the whole damn bottle, taking a shot for every one of the ten days that Catherine had been gone, but his mouth already puckered at the thought. He just wasn't a good enough drunkard to lose himself in booze.

He had tried everything. He had contacted Jace and April, Catherine's agent, the movie studio and even contacted that bastard of a stepfather. God knows how many hours he had spent in that house in the canyons, hoping—no praying—that she would return for some of her things. But she hadn't. And no one knew or was telling where she was. He had even sat down and dialed enough hotels to give his fingers blisters, but none had given him her room. She had covered her tracks well.

At first Sam had believed that Catherine only wanted to be chased. Once he'd found her she would fall into his arms and declare her love for him. He would smile and hold her soft, wonderful body close and tell her that she was his and he would never let go. Then she would smile up at him like she used to. His fist crashed down on the counter. Dammit! He knew she loved him! She had done everything but say so!

He had even found the toothbrushes. Catherine had

carefully taken every one out of the cabinet and thrown them into the trash in the kitchen. It was stupid, but it was the only thing he had to hold on to. A woman who didn't care for her lover and wanted to call off their relationship wouldn't bother wondering what toothbrush her replacement would use. It was the only hope he had.

Slowly, with the help of the others he had contacted, he had pieced together more of her life. The parts she had left out. The private investigator had helped there. It read like a tragedy that no one wanted to admit to. Or a movie that couldn't quite get that old B rating because some of it was so corny and unbelievable. And he marveled at the strength of character that had made her into the warm, wonderful human that she was. It amazed him.

Her life had revealed a pattern to him. She was running away from him because she had been *too* happy. He was sure of that, as stupid as it sounded. All her life, despite her push for success, she had felt that she didn't deserve to reap the rewards her career brought her. She was as much afraid of success and happiness as she craved it. She was like a child who believed that if the gods above saw she was content, they would take away that contentment. As long as she wasn't entirely happy, then she could have the small snatches she came across...then run.

That also explained the two women he always thought she was. One of them was the Catherine everyone knew, especially the press. The other was the little girl who grew into Kitty Slovak, the one who felt she deserved little happiness and knew so very much pain. He now knew why she had left home, such as it was, and her stepfather behind. And why she was so frightened of a dirty old man who believed that he was owed the world. It was revealing to him that she had signed her note with that name, Kitty Slovak. She had been so vulnerable at the time and so very ready to chase those gods away from *him* so he could live in the peace she so desperately craved.

Only he had no peace. Catherine Sinclair, Kitty Slovak: combined, they were both the woman he loved and he was going to get her back if he had to go into a caveman routine and pull her home by her long blond hair!

He downed another tequila.

Somehow Jace had to have the answer. He had to know *something*, *anything* about Catherine and her whereabouts. He had to!

He downed another tequila.

Certainly she would get in touch with Jace. He was her friend and she needed to talk to someone. *Why not me*, his heart cried out, but he didn't have the answer.

He downed another tequila.

"Jace, ol' buddy. You're gonna sing!" He chuckled at his words, only his eyes were almost closed with pain. Picking up the bottle, he walked, swaying slightly, toward the front door. He'd just pay a call to ol' Jace and get some straight answers!

That called for another shot of tequila.

WHEN APRIL OPENED the front door, Sam stumbled in. The bottle was nearly empty and his head was filled with thoughts that made no sense. Except the part that concerned Catherine.

"My God!" she murmured, practically pulling him into the living room. "You're a mess and you smell like a Mexican brewery!"

"Tequila," he slurred. "Jes' a little. Get Jace. I need to talk to Jace."

"He'll be here in a little while, Sam. Meanwhile, go lie down in the guest room and I'll tell you when he comes." Her hands were on her hips, a smile on her face, but concern was deep in her eyes. She had never seen Sam drunk before, and the thought really frightened her.

With April's help, he made it down the wide, tiled hallway to the bedroom, plopping on the bed with a groan and a hand to his head. No matter how hard she tried, April couldn't get one of his feet off the floor and onto the mattress.

"Need it there to steady me," he finally muttered and she left him alone.

Much later he heard voices. Opening his eyes, he saw three Jaces swimming around the room. Damn man wouldn't hold still. Even for a friend! He only heard snatches of conversation.

"Do you think I should call her? She certainly didn't think this would happen!"

"Do you know where she is?"

"Yes, she called yesterday. She's as mixed up as he is." Jace's voice was laden with irony. "She just wanted to know if he was all right."

April's voice murmured something Sam couldn't catch and he was too tired to open his mouth and ask her to repeat it.

Then Jace spoke. "And I don't know if I can talk any sense into either of them. But I'll try. Starting with Catherine."

Sam nodded his head sagely, not realizing it looked as if he was bobbing for apples. His mouth still wouldn't work and all that came out was a muffled groan. But his mind answered. *You tell her, Jace! Go to it!* He turned, groaned and cuddled the pillow to him.

April shook her head as she stared down at Sam. "And to think I once said I wanted to be around when he was finally snared in the net of love. I really thought it'd be fun to have the last laugh," she murmured.

CATHERINE DRIED HER TEARS for the umpteenth time and walked to the door of her bungalow. The knock had been unexpected until she remembered that starting today she had ordered all her meals to be brought at a certain time each day. For more than a week she had gone into the restaurant only sporadically. That wasn't a proper diet. The kitchen and bellboy were ahead of schedule but at least they were here. A small part of her craved to be back in Sam's kitchen where she could concoct new recipes to her heart's delight, but she shoved that thought away.

Her heart did a flip-flop when she answered the door. "Jace!"

His face was stern with lines, his brown eyes seeking hers to make sure she was all right. Then he noticed the tears that glistened in her eyes and knew that she had been crying again. She wiped them quickly away as if ashamed.

"You're in no better shape than Sam is," he said bluntly.

"Oh? And what shape is that?" She turned her back to him, leaving him standing in the doorway. He came in and shut the door with a quiet, definite sound.

"He's at my house, in my guest bedroom, passed out."

She turned quickly. "Drunk?"

"Yes."

"Oh, my God!" she whispered. "He never drinks much! Not even those terrible margaritas he's always making!"

"I know. But he is dead drunk. He's called everyone he can think of to try and find you." Jace came up and held her shoulders, making her look at him. "Please see him, Kitty. He loves you."

"I know," she sniffled, dropping her head to touch his chest. "I know, but it won't work."

"Then tell him so, but at least see him."

"I can't." She shook her head back and forth, and her blond hair spilled on his hands.

"Why not?" he asked, totally exasperated. "For heaven's sake, why not?"

Suddenly her head snapped up and her blue eyes shot sparks. "You wouldn't understand! He's not for me! I'm not good for him!"

"Oh, Catherine, don't go all dramatic on me! This is real life, not some soap opera!"

"Right! And this 'real life' says that it wouldn't work and it's better cutting it off now than attempting to later!" Her hands splayed on his chest. "Please, Jace. Don't make this harder."

He ran a hand through his dark hair. "All right. I don't understand, but I do know that you two have to work it all out yourselves. April and I did, and you will, too, eventually."

"I don't think so."

He gave a hard laugh. "Then you don't know Sam Lewis."

She turned and walked to the back of the small

bungalow, her hands over her stomach. "I think I'm going to have a baby, Jace. Sam's baby."

The tension stretched into unbearable silence and she faced him once again, only to catch his expression of pain. "Oh, Lord," he muttered. "Oh, good Lord."

"And I can't go back to him, Jace. I have my reasons, strange though they may be. He certainly doesn't need me to nurse him back from a hangover, and tomorrow he'll think twice about needing or loving me. Next week he'll almost have forgotten, and by next year, he will hardly remember my name. But I have the future of a child to think of. Just like you do. I have to make sure this baby is loved and cared for, just like you must. I have to. And going back to Sam wouldn't help, it would only make things worse. Soon he'd grow to resent me, and I don't think I could stand that. He's never even mentioned marriage! Not once!"

She paused to take a deep breath before continuing. "Besides, there are things in my past that I don't think he needs to know, but he would if I stayed around. And then we could all sit and watch while he slowly turns against me, hating me more and more every day." She gave a bitter laugh. "Fun at Sam and Kitty's."

Jace looked more puzzled than ever, and she knew she would never be able to tell him that her greatest fear was that Sam would find out she was a big fraud, a nothing. Her stepfather and the writing on the walls could confirm that. And she didn't want to be there when it happened. "But, Kitty, those are all things that could be worked out."

"No." She shook her head, the blueness of her eyes showing the determination she felt. "Never in a million years, Jace. Never." She choked on the last words.

Jace took her in his arms, cradling her against the pain he knew she felt. "All right, Kitty. All right. I won't tell him where you are," he crooned as she cried again. Who knew whether or not she was right? He only knew he wanted to stop her hurt.

13

CATHERINE SAT in the reception area of her agent's office, her legs crossed, her hands quietly in her lap. Her large-brimmed white hat hid half her face from the receptionist, but the young girl gave an envious glance every minute or so, anyway.

She had already been kept waiting five minutes, but it didn't matter. She had other, more important things to think about. She shifted her legs and recrossed them.

Now she knew for certain that she was pregnant. A child grew in her, depended upon her for life, and she had known it earlier with such a certainty that it was frightening. She had no experience with pregnancy, no vast knowledge to pull from, but she knew. According to her calculations she should be six weeks pregnant. An at-home test confirmed it and an appointment with a doctor tomorrow would establish it as fact.

She smiled. Never in her life had she taken such good care of herself as she had in the past few weeks. She took her vitamins regularly, ate three well-balanced meals a day and got a minimum of eight hours of sleep a night. She walked the grounds of the hotel for exercise and sometimes went into the hotel gym to ride their exercise bike. This baby was going to have the best start that she and God could give it.

These past weeks had also been a private time. Time

to withdraw, regroup and take a look at herself. Something she had never done properly before.

It was ironic in a way. For the past two weeks she had gone through such inner turmoil, forcing herself to see, really see, herself and the goals she wanted to strive for in life. She had finally blended Catherine Sinclair and Kitty Slovak together, and she was proud of herself and her accomplishments for the first time in her life. She had balanced her assets against her deficits, just like a bookkeeper, and realized that she was in the black. And now that she knew what she really wanted, she couldn't have it. The love she had for Sam was all that was important, but she found she couldn't go back to him because she was pregnant. The man she had fallen in love with was the perfect choice, but the time was wrong. She wasn't the perfect choice for him.

He would hate her for boxing him in this way. He was neither suited for nor had asked to be a father. No, it would be a forced marriage for him when marriage had never before been mentioned. She could have cornered him into doing the right thing because he would have felt responsible enough for both of them.

She rested her hand on her stomach, thinking of the small baby there. This child was going to have all the love and time and attention she could lavish. She didn't know how, but she was going to be a model mother. She was going to give this child, their child, everything she had never had. Cookies and milk in the afternoon, lots of hugs and kisses and a sunny house that rang with laughter and love. It was her second chance to prove she was worth something.

And she had made another decision about her life-style

and career. One that she would discuss with Tommy today.

"Miss Sinclair? Right this way," the young receptionist said as she ushered her toward the large, walnut-stained double doors. The receptionist appraised the jade-green silk suit and the crisp white blouse with a knowing eye, realizing it probably cost more than her own weekly salary. Some people had fortune and fame handed to them on a silver platter, while others had to work for it, she seemed to be thinking.

Catherine smiled knowingly. She'd seen that look before.

"Catherine, baby!" Tommy came around the desk and met her halfway across the room. His style was strictly Los Angeles, a pair of hand-tailored dark slacks with a dark silk shirt, and the required two heavy gold chains around his stubby neck. He was an almost attractive man who always looked as if he had just completed a huge meal and needed to unbuckle his belt before his stomach ached. "Good of you to come on such short notice."

"No problem, Tommy. I needed to talk with you, anyway," she said quietly, finally pulling her hand back from his damp grasp.

He showed her to the Morris chair, the seat of honor, and moved around the desk to sit in his own large executive chair. Giving a sigh of contentment, he folded his hands together and looked at her. A delightful beam seemed to light his eyes. "I've got a contract for you that will knock your socks off. Besides that, we've managed to get you an option on a new film. That means you're assured of doing two films and really getting your feet wet in the movies." He grinned even more. "A whole new career."

"That's wonderful, Tommy, except that I don't want an option on anything. I'll make *Oklahoma* because I don't think we can get out of that contract, but then I'm retiring for a while. A long while."

His face dropped. "But you can't do that!" He leaned forward. "Maybe I didn't make myself clear. Instead of one movie, which may or may not make it, you can get signed for two!" He leaned back and beamed again, certain that she would respond the way he wanted.

Catherine smiled. "I understand. Only, I don't want to do two. I don't even want to do one, but since I've committed myself, I'll do it. Then I'm retiring." Now it was her turn to lean back. She smiled again. She had thought this decision out, considering the pros and cons over and over in her head. Her body had been telling her that she didn't want to continue working, but her mind had been on automatic, ignoring all the signs. Now, after weeks of soul-searching, she had finally made the decision to retire. And in making that decision she felt free, almost weightless with relief. Just saying it aloud was the greatest release of her life. She had been right. She wanted out.

Tommy leaned forward again, a frown making his whole face sag. "Is it because of this guy, Sam Lewis? The one you stayed with when your house was burglarized?"

Her brows shot up. Even his name still made her heartbeat accelerate. "No." Her voice was firm and quick and sure.

"Okay then, stay here," he muttered, stepping from behind his desk and quickly walking toward a side door that Catherine presumed led to another office. "If I can't convince you, maybe he can." He opened it and slipped through, shutting it quickly behind him.

Catherine almost wanted to laugh. Poor Tommy! He had gone to bring out the big guns and ask other agents what to do! It had been such a relief to state her decision out loud that Catherine could laugh at almost anything.

A smile was still tugging at her lips when she heard the door reopen. But the prickles on her neck told her that it wasn't Tommy who had entered.

Sam stood just inside the room, his arms by his sides, his facial expression one of a man in great pain.

Catherine stood and faced him, her hands clenching as she stared back. He was devouring her with his eyes, and her whole body seemed to lean toward him, responding to his look as surely as if he had touched her. She took a step forward and so did he, then they both stopped and stared at each other.

"I told Tommy earlier that you needed me here to guard you against relatives who might try to barge in. He believed me enough to let me wait in the other room." The muscles of his jaw jumped. "If he didn't let me see you I was going to accost you in the elevator on your way out."

Her heart was racing with a giddiness that she couldn't control. She drank in his lean strength, her glance barely settling on his unsmiling face, his dark hair, his broad shoulders, his lean hips, his large but gentle hands that were clenched, like hers.

A watchful expression passed over his face and she realized that he had purposely set this up. "Sam, why?" she whispered through her tightened throat.

Her words released him from his stiff position. He walked toward her, his every step showing his determination. "Because I love you and this time you're going to listen to me." His voice was gruff. "I was too easy with you, trying to bring you gently along to my way of thinking without harming your ego. Well, now lady, I'm gonna hurt your ego until you cry 'uncle' because I'm not letting you go again. Ever."

She shook her head back and forth, denying his words even before he said them. She took a step back. "You don't understand."

"I don't have to. You're the one who has to understand and give me the credit for not being a dumbbell." His voice was almost a growl.

"I never thought you were that." Her voice was low, filled with emotion that she could barely contain.

"Yes, you did," he corrected. "You thought I wasn't smart enough to know the lady I loved. You thought I was some damn fool in love with a ghost of a woman, someone I only knew through the media and records. You didn't give me credit for knowing the real woman. The woman who is a beautiful, crazy, wild and very sad blend of Catherine Sinclair and Kitty Slovak."

"You don't know..." Her voice drifted off as she slowly absorbed the truth of his words. He had said he loved her....

"Yes, I do, so there's no more running for you to do." His voice was strong, his eyes caring, caressing her. "I know about you, about your past and your present, and God help me, your future."

He wasn't lying. She could see it in his eyes. He knew everything about her—everything except the baby— and he still wanted her! She searched for pity but she couldn't find any. A sorrow seemed to etch his eyes but there was also an almost overwhelming abundance of love. Love for her.

"My..." She couldn't continue. The words would

make him hate her forever and she just couldn't do that. She needed to keep something of him.

"Your weak, pitiful stepfather blamed you for constantly 'tempting' him," he stated calmly. "And you finally ran away from home, only to find out that most of the men you met did the very same thing. From the time you were fifteen, men were blaming you for what they felt and you childishly accepted their blame." His brows rose. "Right?"

Catherine couldn't answer him, she could only stare.

Sam continued. "Only now you're years older and you still believe the same thing. I should have taken you over my knee and spanked you like I promised. That's what a young girl might believe, but that's *not* the way it was, and you should know better now. Had you had any kind of a solid upbringing, you would have realized it, too." He took another step toward her, only this time she didn't back away.

"Well, I'm here to teach you differently, lady. I'm here to tell you that I want you so badly I ache, but it's *my* wants that make me ache, not yours. It's *my* needs that keep me awake at night, not yours." He took another step until he was just inches away from her. His eyes burned holes in hers as his words branded her soul and made her believe. "But it's going to be *my* love that you share. I'll just have to teach you, that's all."

She didn't know how she took that small step into his arms, but then she didn't care. He held her so tightly that his arms became bands of steel around her shoulders, but she didn't care. He was here. He loved her, he wanted her, and he was here.

"Oh, Sam." She breathed his name with a catch in her throat. "I love you so much."

They kissed as if each were succor for the other, their hands pressing, touching, holding to ensure that they were where they should be, where they wanted to be, in each other's arms.

His breath was ragged, his heart pumping as if he were ten men. "Catherine Sinclair or Kitty Slovak, I don't care which, but you're marrying me as soon as it can be arranged. I'm not letting you out of my sight again until I know I can trust you to come home to me without my coercing you into it."

"I will. I promise, teacher." She smiled up at him then and the smile wrapped around his heart and gave a tug so hard that it brought tears to his eyes.

"No more arguments? No fights?" he asked huskily.

"No arguments. No fights," she promised.

"Why the change, Catherine?" His frown showed his worry. He had not been expecting immediate capitulation. She chuckled, then kissed the tip of his very stubborn chin. Sam continued unperturbed, "When Jace came back from wherever you were, he said that there was no way he could convince you to contact me. What happened between then and now that could change your mind?"

"Because you're right. I was running. I thought your love was frightening to me. I had never experienced anything like it before and I didn't know what else to do. Then I found out that I was in love with you, and that scared me even more. And I was afraid of what you would think of me when you found out about my stepfather badgering me until I had to run away from home." She sighed, resting her head against the firmness of his chest. "But it was nothing compared to the way I felt without you," she admitted.

"Then why didn't you come back to me?" His arms encircled her waist, his grip still punishing. He knew all about her and he didn't care. She could speak the truth now.

"Because I've carried around this load of guilt for so long that I had allowed it to grow out of proportion." She looked up at him, a small frown between her brows. His smile of love wiped it away. "I should have done as you suggested and talked it out, but I couldn't seem to do it. I thought I needed time to sort things out. Then, weeks passed and it was harder...."

His arms tightened once more. "Didn't you realize I wouldn't have cared? I don't give a damn what our pasts are; they're behind us now and we can start fresh together."

For the first time, her eyes twinkled mischievously. "Right, teach," she murmured huskily, loving the feel of his hands on her back, his thighs against hers.

"And stop calling me teacher," he ordered.

"Why?" Her gaze grew wide. "It fits so well."

"Because I didn't really teach you anything. You taught me."

"Oh, no, Sam." She chuckled at his frown. "You taught me: one, how to be a friend; two, what it was like to be loved, really loved; three..." Her voice drifted off as he gave her parted lips a kiss.

"And you taught me," he said roughly. "You taught me just how boring the life of a swinging single could be."

Her hands played in his hair. "Does that mean you don't mind about those toothbrushes?"

He chuckled. "Those toothbrushes in the trash were the only things that gave me hope in my bleakest moments. If you hadn't done that, I might not have stayed sane enough to stand here with you now. I kept thinking that you had to love me or you wouldn't have bothered throwing them out."

Her shining blue eyes twinkled through the tears that refused to go away. "I gave myself away?"

"Thank you for that," he said, his voice a low growl.

She hesitated.

"What's on your mind, Catherine. Out with it."

"Will I have to work for a while to support us?"

"Never," he said quickly. "But you'll have to cut out buying those commercial paintings every time you turn around."

"It was just one and it was a memento, to remind me of our day at the beach," she protested.

"Now you won't need any more mementos. I'll take you every week. Better still, we'll buy a house on the beach. I may not be as wealthy as you are, but I'm certainly no pauper." He leaned back to look down at her, his brown eyes crinkling. "What do you think?"

She grinned. "Great, as long as it has plenty of bedrooms and a large patio."

"Your wish..." He hesitated. "It might mean you'll have to drive a long way to work."

"Would you mind my not working? Ever? After this picture, I mean."

His grin lit up his face and her insides. "Not at all, lady. Not at all."

"Good," she finally confessed. "Lately, every time I think of singing to a large crowd, my voice tightens up and I become frightened again."

"You don't have to worry about that. I'd rather have you home and in my arms all the time. But, if and when you're ready to hit the road again, I'll be waiting."

That was when she really realized he did love her. He loved her. For the first time in years she felt cleansed, and it was all because of Sam. Wonderful, sweet, bull-headed Sam.

They kissed again, only this time the urgency wasn't there. It was a pledge. One for a long life of happiness.

"Bingo," he whispered when they parted. "I got the brass ring."

Catherine chuckled throatily. "And you've also got a hot-tub."

Sam's brows rose. "I do? Where?"

"I ordered it to be delivered tomorrow. That's so you won't have to go to a 'friend's' house to enjoy it."

"Remind me to explain the word 'budget' to you as soon as we get home," he said with a grin.

"That *was* going to be my parting gift to you," she explained, her blue eyes filled with mirth. "But since you're so insistent on our staying together—"

"Getting married," he inserted roughly.

"Getting married," she finished. "It's just as well. That way I'll know where you are at night."

His grin widened. "Oh, darling, are you ever full of surprises," he murmured.

Her blue eyes lit with mischievous lights. "Sam, my love, do I have some surprises for you," she crooned, tilting her neck so he could nibble better. "You ain't heard nothin' yet."

You're invited to accept 4 books and a surprise gift **Free!**

Acceptance Card

Mail to: **Harlequin Reader Service®**

In the U.S.
2504 West Southern Ave.
Tempe, AZ 85282

In Canada
P.O. Box 2800, Postal Station A
5170 Yonge Street
Willowdale, Ontario M2N 6J3

YES! Please send me 4 free Harlequin Temptation® novels and my free surprise gift. Then send me 4 brand new novels every month as they come off the presses. Bill me at the low price of $1.99 each ($1.95 in Canada)—a 13% saving off the retail price. There are no shipping, handling or other hidden costs. There is no minimum number of books I must purchase. I can always return a shipment and cancel at any time. Even if I never buy another book from Harlequin, the 4 free novels and the surprise gift are mine to keep forever.

142 BPX-BPGE

Name	(PLEASE PRINT)	

Address		Apt. No.

City	State/Prov.	Zip/Postal Code

This offer is limited to one order per household and not valid to present subscribers. Price is subject to change.

ACHT-SUB-1

COMING IN SEPTEMBER
THE...

- **Win a Rolls-Royce™ (or $100,000 cash)**
  - **Or a trip to Paris**
  - **Or a mink coat**

See September books
for more details.